I0728468

All I Want For Christmas Is A Mermaid

LIANA BROOKS

OTHER WORKS

ALL I WANT FOR CHRISTMAS

All I Want For Christmas Is A Werewolf
All I Want For Christmas Is A Reaper
All I Want For Christmas Is A Gargoyle
All I Want For Christmas Is A Cryptid
All I Want For Christmas Is A Mermaid

FLEET OF MALIK

Bodies In Motion
Change of Momentum

HEROES AND VILLAINS

Even Villains Fall In Love
Even Villains Go To The Movies
Even Villains Have Interns
Even Villains Play The Hero (omnibus)
The Polar Terror

TIME AND SHADOWS

The Day Before
Convergence Point
Decoherence

SHORTER WORKS

Darkness and Good
Escape: The Liana Brooks Sci Fi Collection
Fey Lights
If You Give A Skeleton A 3D Printer
Prime Sensations
The Complete Inklet Collection
The Price Of The Mountain Lily

Find other works by the author at www.lianabrooks.com

All I Want For Christmas Is A

Mermaid

LIANA BROOKS

AUSTRALIA

Copyright © 2025 Liana Brooks

All rights reserved. No part of this book may be reproduced in any form or by any electronic or mechanical means, including information storage and retrieval systems, without permission in writing from the publisher, except by a reviewer, who may quote brief passages in a review.

This is a work of fiction. All characters, organisations and events are the author's creation, or are used fictitiously.

Without in any way limiting the author's exclusive rights under copyright, no part of this book may be used or reproduced in any manner for the purpose of training artificial intelligence (AI) technologies or systems without express contractual permission from the author.

Paperback ISBN: 978-1-923305-07-6
Hardcover ISBN: 978-1-923305-10-6
eBook ISBN: 9798232477158

www.inkprintpress.com

National Library of Australia Cataloguing-in-Publication Data
Brooks, Liana 1982—
All I Want For Christmas Is A Mermaid
154 p.   cm.
ISBN: 9798232477158
Inkprint Press, Canberra, Australia
1. Fiction—Romance—Paranormal—General 2. Fiction—Fantasy—Paranormal 3. Fiction—Holidays

Summary: A cruise ship off the coast of Australia is the perfect place for LJ to hide from her abusive family—until she takes a job as a birthday party mermaid and crashes head-first into her past.

First Edition: December 2025

Cover design © Inkprint Press

This book was published on Ngunnawal country. The publisher would like to acknowledge the people who have told their stories here for countless generations.

To everyone who is working to make the future of their dreams.

Special thanks to Amy and Derek, my twins. I couldn't do this without you.

ALL I WANT FOR CHRISTMAS IS A MERMAID

SMOKE HUNG OVER MY HEAD IN THE RAFTERS OVER THE BAR IN Jenni's Spot like a bad memory. Never mind that indoor smoking had been illegal in Louisiana for nigh on forty years, it was there. Clinging on like regrets, bad dreams, and the smell of cheap beer. Everything made it clear, this was a place where nightmares belonged.

Jenni's Spot was a truck stop in the middle of the swamps somewhere between New Orleans and Biloxi, down south of I-90 tucked between the pearls.

That'd be the Pearl River and the Old Pearl River if you were a mapmaker. For everybody local it was a joke. And not the kind you'd tell in church.

Not that any of the varmints currently clogging the bar had been to church in recent memory. Not unless drinking on St. Paddy's Day counted. We weren't Irish down here, not outside the Irish Bayou at least, but we drank like the fishes in the bayou at Polecat Bend.

"Lainey Jane!" Jenni's smoke-stained voice rang out from the gloom of her office. "Get these tables cleared out! There's a wreck an' all the traffic's coming our way!"

"On it!" I hollered back over the strained music coming from aging speakers.

"Wish you was on me," one of the regulars said, laughing as he sloshed swamp hooch in a cup that probably hadn't been truly clean in over a decade.

I was already turning to give him the dismissal he so desperately wanted when a large hand pulled me back against a warm wall.

"You lookin' for a fight, Willard?" a deliciously deep voice that was pure Cajun asked as the scent of dark chocolate and cold mornings on the river wrapped around me. "Miss Lainey Jane is mine."

For a moment time seemed to freeze and I could picture myself turning, smiling, feeling warm and loved and wanted in a way I'd never been. Wanted for myself and not for the work I could do for someone else. Wanted because the man standing behind me actually meant what he said.

The vision snapped with Willard's snicker.

"Miss Lainey Jane is her own damn woman," I said, pushing the hand away, and turned to glare at Marcus Dupre.

My glare bounced off an unsinkable Cajun man. Six four in bare feet, shoulders like a linebacker, muscles cut like he was posing for a magazine in the morning, chocolate brown eyes with flecks of ocean blue, sun-tanned skin, and rich brown hair every girl in the parish wanted to touch, Marcus "Mako" Dupre belonged to the sprawling clan of Dupres who were spread up and down the rivers like they owned them. His grandma was called Queen and she lived up to it. The whole passel of them were nothing but trouble.

This one though... I thought we'd seen the back of him years ago but, like another round of bad news, he kept showing up. He wasn't cruel, not like my father or brothers, but he was a Dupre. That meant he could go from flashing a killer smile to simply killing someone with the blink of an eye. The whole family was that way: you were either on their side, or you were an enemy.

I'd never known what he saw me as, so I stayed safe and kept my distance. Even now, when the chill of the winter air wafting through the front door made me want to curl up in his warm arms. Perfect proof that I'd been working too long and had lost my ever-lovin' mind.

His smile was as slow and seductive as a swaying snake. "You wound me, cher. You could be mine."

"Yours?" I pushed away from him, quietly looking for the nearest steak knife. A Dupre usually needed to be losing a lot of blood before they remembered to listen. "I'm surprised you even remember my name. Must be why you forgot I don't like the idea of being owned. Or was it because the last time you saw me was seven years ago?" The last time I'd talked to him was the year we graduated, right before Marcus vanished in a wave of rumors. Maybe he went to college; more likely he went to prison. Wherever it'd been, he was back.

Charming as he was, my future plans did not include getting entangled with another powerful, capricious family. The Mako could hunt all he wanted, I'd be the ornery octopus slapping him if he got too close.

"Last time I saw you was in my bed last night." Stormy, ocean-flecked brown eyes looked me up and down, taking in the tiny cutoff denim shorts and too-small black t-shirt that were the Jenni's official uniform for the ladies.

"In your dreams maybe."

"And what good dreams dey were. You were singing me a siren song."

"I hope it led you to a watery grave." I grabbed an empty plate from Willard's table and gave Marcus the cold shoulder as I headed for the kitchen. Let him look. It was the last eyeful of me he was ever going to get.

I made Wyatt take the swamp prince's table. The tips would be good either way. Marcus liked anything with nipples, everyone said so. It was the only reason he'd never been caught wrestling gator for anything more than a roadside sport.

It sounded mean, but it was true. On our sixth grade field trip to the wildlife center he'd been caught staring at a manatee and all he said was, "I like her curves."

In school he'd been my Designated Crush.[1] Not that I was alone in that. Everyone had liked him, boys, girls, and anyone in between. Marcus Dupre had a smile that could melt ice off a nun and a voice smoother than the finest Kentucky bourbon. He was hot, but he was the kind of weird you'd have to be crazy to love. And I wasn't crazy.

Nobody had time for that, least of all me.

Not anymore.

FOUR HOURS LATER THE DINNER RUSH WAS CLOSING TO A CRAWL, Willard was on cheap beer number nine and singing tunelessly with a buddy who'd stumbled in already drunk an hour ago, and I found myself reaching for my apron strings.

This was it. I was really doing it.

"Lainey Jane!" Cook hollered. "Order up for table five!"

---

[1] That person you tell everyone you like when they ask who your crush is because you're too worried, busy, stressed, or ace to actually have a crush. I wasn't asexual, but I also didn't have time for falling in love. I was too busy trying to survive.

"On it."

Willard gave me a look he probably thought was flirtatious.

I dropped fried catfish and okra at table five in front of some truckers complaining about the wrecks on the highway and headed for the back room next to Jenni's main office.

"Whatchya doing, Lainey Jane?" the boss asked as I took my apron off and dropped it in the washing bin for the closing crew to handle.

"Clocking out, boss." My shoulders tensed at what I knew was coming. "It's after midnight."

"Clocking out?" Jenni scoffed, her usually bored voice turning mean. "You think you can clock out now?"

"I've been here over ten hours," I said, eyes on the dirty, boot-scuffed, mud-stained brown floor. "I pulled doubles yesterday, the day before, and all last week."

"Is this about tips?" Jenni demanded. "It's only fair we divvy 'em up like that. Everybody oughts to get paid."

I should have let it go, it wouldn't matter in the morning, but I couldn't. Keeping my voice calm I said, "Wyatt and I are the ones waiting tables on minimum wage. Cookie gets double what I make even with my tips!" My ears burned in humiliation and rage I couldn't contain.

Jenni stood up. She actually moved out of her rolling chair and away from whatever online game she was addicted to this week. "You listen here, Lil Miss Too Big For Her Britches, there's another wreck westbound on the ninety. All them truckers are goin' to be comin' in here. We're 'bout to be busier than a cook at a crawfish boil. If you want this job tomorrow, you're going to stay to close."

I turned, eyes snapping up meet her gaze. "Then cut me my pay."

"What?" Jenni blinked. "What did you say?"

"I said pay me what you owe me, 'cause I'm going home." There was no air left in the room, only smoke and the smell of rancid grease from the kitchen. My heart raced with fear. And hope.

I could do this.

I *had* to do this.

Jenni's penciled-in eyebrows climbed up to her bottle-blonde bangs. "Lainey Jane I thought you were better than that. Better than those good-for-nothing brothers of yours. If you don't have a job tomorrow, who's going to pay the bills at your house? Heaven knows your daddy ain't kept a job in his life. How're they going to eat if you storm off like this?"

The bar outside had gone quiet, all ears on us.

Licking my lips nervously I stepped closer so I could whisper to Jenni, "Please? My period started. I already bled through my panties. I need to get home to get changed."

Jenni's lips puckered in a scowl. She looked me up and down.

"I paid all the bills today. I need my paycheck so I can go get pads. Lady stuff. You know?" I looked to her for sympathy.

"Uh, fine." She rolled her eyes and stalked back into her office.

The noise of the bar resumed as Jenni popped the cash drawer open and she counted out my week's pay. Nine hundred dollars, all mine.

She put three hundred back. "For the tips you're missing," she said, holding out the cash. "And you best be here ten ay-em for opening and plan to stay to lock up. Or I really will go hire someone else. I'm taking a risk, letting someone like you work here."

"Yes, ma'am, I know." I took the cash, glanced over it to make sure it was really there, and nodded. "Thank you so much. I'll never forget this."

Ever.

That was a threat, not a promise.

In the tiny employee bathroom I changed into black sweat pants and a faded t-shirt with a yellow water dragon swimming past a mermaid's underwater palace, a gift from a customer years ago. The denim shorts and work shirt were Jenni's, technically, so I dropped those in the laundry bin with my apron. I wasn't letting her charge me with theft.

No one noticed as I slipped out the back door. There'd been street lamps out here years ago when Jenni's Spot was new. They were overgrown by kudzu vines now.

If it weren't for the flickering neon sign at the front of the building, anyone driving past the gravel lot would think this place was abandoned most days. Tonight there was the sound of trucks parking on the far side of the building, hollers combined with the sound of air brakes. An owl soared silently overhead.

Down the way someone screamed along with a country song about lost love and starting over.

"Lainey Jane." The sexiest Cajun accent ever to exist wound its way out of the shadows like a cottonmouth hunting for dinner.

Marcus stood there in the shadows between the dumpster and his bright yellow pickup with the vanity license plate that read *YumYum.*[2]

It hit me, all over again, this was the best I was ever expected to have. Some feral Cajun boy flirting with me between the grease pit and the trash pile because I was the prettiest thing with two legs nearby.

"What do you want?"

"Is there something wrong with a neighborly hello?" he asked as he strolled toward me.

"You get close enough to touch me again, I'm going to find a rock big enough to knock some sense into you." My

---

[2] Definitely a reference to the rumor that sharks like the color yellow and nothing else. Definitely nothing else.

voice was flat. Not with fear, with rage. I was angry at Marcus, and the owl, and my family, and the whole world who dealt me the worst hand every day and expected me to be grateful for the crumbs.

"You driving home?" Marcus stopped a safe distance away. I would still like a few thousand more miles between us, but that wasn't going to happen today.

I lifted one shoulder in a shrug. "Maybe. Maybe not. Don't see how it's any of your business either way."

"Was just being neighborly. Figured I'd drive behind you so I can tow that ol' thing once it finally dies on you." He nodded to the powder-blue POS that was older than I was by a decade.

"She gets me where I need to go."

"I could get you there too." If innuendo was a subtle hint, this was whatever the opposite of innuendo was. "Make all your dreams come true."

I rolled my eyes in the dark. "Sure thing. Next time I see you, you can buy me a drink."

"Promise?"

"Scout's honor." I'd never been a scout of any kind, but that didn't matter. Marcus, like the rest of this armpit of a town, were all going to be a bad nightmare in twenty-four hours. "See you around, Marcus."

I locked my car doors as soon as I got in and drove down to the gas station at the edge of the highway. I lived one exit to the west. I drove that way along the side road until I was out of range of the gas station cameras, pulled off road into a clump of trees, and walked to the trunk of my car, heart racing.

This was it. Today was the day. I was finally, finally doing it.

In the trunk was everything I owned. My bright yellow suitcase, my college diploma that I'd earned from six years of online classes, my new SIM card for my phone. I popped out the old SIM card, the one I'd had since I got my first phone as a hand-me-down at age nine, and put the new one in place.

When I hit the entrance to the highway, I went east.

Next stop: Atlanta.

THREE YEARS LATER

MY PHONE BUZZED IN MY HIP POCKET AS I FINISHED FOLDING MY laundry on the tiny bunk bed I called home eleven months of the year. Rocking as the floor of the cruise ship swayed with the tides, I pulled my phone out for a look. The cheerful yellow case with me in my full Moonlight Mermaid regalia from last year's show brought a smile to my face as I checked the caller ID.

A 0239 number, which meant Wagga Wagga and probably a spam call. I hit the block button.

There was another notification on my phone, this one from my memories.

With a tap I opened it and saw pictures from two years ago when I'd first moved to Australia. My chestnut brown hair with coppery red highlights was in curls, I wore a red Atlanta Dream[3] t-shirt, and the look of someone who hadn't slept in thirty-six hours because I hadn't.

But I was smiling.

I was so proud of that smile.

------

[3] Atlanta Dream is the WNBA team in Atlanta. My first pay check that I kept to myself I went to one of their games to celebrate.

I'd earned it. I'd fought for it. I'd spent the seven[4] years after high school working in hell so I could pay my family's bills and afford the occasional college credit. All those long shifts and extra gig work had bought me a degree in the hospitality industry and opened the door to a better job in Atlanta.

But that had only been a stepping stone. A place to give me an address so I could get a passport without taking a beating for "wasting money" or "being selfish". Then I put over eight thousand miles between me and my nightmare -inducing childhood.

Three years after fleeing the backwater swamps of Louisiana I was stable, healthy, and feeling like a whole human being. Part of that probably had to do with the fact that I was getting four weeks off from work, paid.

Checking one last time to make sure everything I owned was squeezed into my yellow backpack, I headed out of my cabin and to the main deck where Amelia was waiting to give me a ride out of Sydney Harbor. We'd been in port for four hours, but the promenade was already crowded with new faces of eager explorers off to adventure for the summer holidays.

Or hols if you were an Aussie.

The Merry Mermaid was one of five ships belonging to Alonnah Cruise Lines, and she was the largest. Capable of circumnavigating Oceania, the *Mermaid* regularly sailed as far south as Auckland and as far north as Okinawa.[5]

Neither were places I could have found on a map four years ago. Now I could recite fun facts about them and identify which sea we were in by the shells on sale at the

---

[4] It took me a year of working every job I could get to save enough money to even start college, and then six years to finish college.

[5] Auckland is in New Zealand, Okinawa is the southern tip of Japan.

Mermaid Trinket kiosk by the mermaid show where I worked.

Right now the promenade featured miniature Sydney Opera Houses and cowry shells commonly found in the waters of Sydney, Australia.

"LJ!" Kilee Moyle waved at me from the center of a crowd of googly-eyed tourists that smelled of sunscreen and forgotten deodorant. Kilee was dressed for work in the same green wig with a clamshell crown and glittering green dress that I often wore. In front of her was an array of sparkling cards, the kind that left you contaminated with glitter for a fortnight.[6]

Swallowing a put-upon sigh, I walked over. "Hello, Marvelous Minerva!" I said in my best Aussie deckhand voice.

"Everyone," Kilee said, "this is LJ, one of our happy helpers here on *The Merry Mermaid*. She does everything to make your day extra awesome! She's about to go for some shore leave, should we see her future for her?"

"Yes!" several small children squealed in delight.

Across the table with the *Marvelous Minerva Seas All*[7] sign, Kilee grinned at me.

Brett must have been busy because it was his day to have his fortune told to make all the suckers—excuse me—*tourists* pay good money to have a fake magician read their future in the cards.[8]

---

[6] A fortnight is two weeks and a commonly used saying in Australia. When I moved here I thought it was only a video game.

[7] Yes, the typo is intentional. No, that didn't stop my eye from twitching every time I saw it.

[8] They weren't tarot cards. They'd been tarot cards once upon a time and then a passenger threw a fit. Now they were *Minerva's Lucky Life Deck* and they sold for $50 AUD at the shop next door. For a cool $100 you could buy the deck in the color of your choice and a matching box covered in rhinestones.

Reminding myself that my employers were very kindly paying for me to have a four-week holiday on land, I put on my bright Happy Helper smile.[9] "All right." I tapped three of the cards fanned out in front of me at random. "What's my future hold, oh Marvelous Minerva?"

Kilee did her act, waving her hands over the cards and pulling them out with mysterious looks. "Ooo! Your future is bright!" She flipped over the sun card for everyone to ogle.

Drawing the second card, her eyes widened dramatically and she pronounced, "You will find magic and mermaids!" She showed us the second card, the mermaid, which was usually the third and led to a spiel about the mermaid shows all guests were encouraged to attend.

"True love is waiting for you!" Kilee assured as she flipped over the final card.

The Lovers card stared back at me, with a black-haired man who reminded me far too much of a man I hadn't seen in three years. I'd never see Marcus Dupre again in person, but he seemed determined to haunt me all the same.

Blame it on the last night's late conversation with my friends; we'd been talking about who we'd left behind, and I'd spun a tale of an ex-boyfriend who was almost something more. Of course Kilee would remember that. She was the only one besides me who'd stayed sober.

My cheeks burned and I'd bet money they were bright red.

"Enjoy your vacation!" Kilee's smile was all-seeing, all-knowing, and all-teasing. Of course she'd set me up like that. "It looks there's someone waiting for you on land."

I was never going to live down the rumors of my early crush. But I kept my Happy Helper smile firmly in place

---

[9] My other default was Mysterious Mermaid and I saved that one for when I was swimming in the mermaid show.

for the crowd.

"Thanks!" I waved at the tourists. "Enjoy your sweet sail!"

Working my way through the crowd, I found Amelia by the back stairs that only crew were allowed to use. My bunkmate and fellow mermaid had naturally blonde hair and dazzling blue eyes. She was outgoing, friendly, and flirtatious. It was easy to get along with her.

We'd bonded over a love of the TV show *All These Broken Seasons* and happily spent our working hours together tempting tourists to their financial doom.[10]

"What did you tell Kilee?" I asked as Amelia and I hustled down the narrow stairs to our exit. "She gave me the most mixed-up fortune for the hols."

"I only said I had a surprise for you!"

I rubbed my hands together like I was praying. "Please be ten million dollars. Please be ten million dollars."

"I wish!" Amelia laughed. "Even better..." She stopped at the platform and looked around to make sure no one was nearby. "...I got you a gig! Shh!" She held a finger to her lips. "Not here!" With a nod to the security cameras, she hustled me off the ship.

Iron-willed control kept me from bursting with questions until we were safely into Amelia's little ocean-blue Holden Captiva that was waiting for us in the employee car park.

"Spill!" I demanded as I buckled into where the driver's side belonged. Two years out of the States and I still found it weird that the wheel was on the wrong side of the car.

"So," Amelia turned the car on and the water engine purred like a kitten, "I know you planned on just bumming

---

[10] Pictures with the mermaids started at \$200 and a swim lesson with me while I used my Cajun creole accent cost \$800. Lots of people paid for that and fell in love Evangeline Mire, the gator-wrestling mermaid from the bayou.

at some beach house for the hols, but, a friend of the family reached out to me and asked if I'd be willing to come be a mermaid for her niece's birthday party. But, there's some other stuff I need to take care of." She nodded to the back seat where her bags and an extra green box were sitting.

"Oh." That didn't sound very exciting. "I mean, sure. What day is it?"

Amelia's grin grew wider as we merged onto the A4 highway. "This is the best part, it's a three day celebration, and then we get two weeks in the guest house."

"The guest house where?"

"The family owns a big block of land along the coast. Like, someone's grandpappy hit the lotto or something, came here, and bought up a town basically. Every house belongs to a cousin or some such. And one of the big houses has a two-bedroom guest house by the small pool—"

"Small pool?"

"The house has three pools." Amelia's grin put the sun to shame. "The guest house is isolated from the main house and has a small pool. You go. You play mermaid for a little girl. You eat cake. You get to stay there instead of renting a place until mid-January. I'll come catch up with you as soon as I can."

"I thought you were going to Canberra[11] to be with your mum?"

Amelia shrugged. "I mean, I will. But they're paying good money for this. This other thing should be done by tomorrow, so you can go tonight, get started, and I'll pop in tomorrow arvo.[12] No worries!"

---

[11] That'd be the capital of Australia. Although I hear it's nicer than living in Washington D.C.

[12] Arvo is Aussie slang for afternoon.

Mentally I ran the math. I was used to making decent money these days. The cruise line paid me a baseline salary of three hundred and fifty dollars a day, American, which was something a little above forty dollars an hour. Every mermaid show I did earned extra, and then I got a percentage of the appearance fees so every picture and swim class gave me thirty percent.

I'd run the numbers once on how much cruise tickets cost versus the number of passengers and I'm not sure how the bosses were making money. But, considering where we cruised around Oceania and the South China Sea, I was willing to bet their profit came from undisclosed shipping. Something I was very sure not to ask questions about. I didn't even let myself think about it hard. Maybe that was my bayou roots showing, but I'd lose my work visa if I got caught up in that nonsense, so I kept well away from it.

"How much?" I asked, breaking through Amelia's chatter about the size of the guest house and the ocean views from the balcony.

"You're going to love this."

"I better."

"Fifteen grand a day."

My eyes went wide. "That's a month's worth of pay!" Even on my best months I rarely made more than thirteen thousand a month. I grabbed my phone to see what the Aussie-American dollar exchange rates were. The Aussie dollar couldn't possibly be that worthless, but that was the only I way I could explain someone paying us close to thirty grand, American, for three days of work.

Amelia nodded eagerly. "Every day we show up to play mermaids, fifteen thousand smackaroos."

"That's not a word."

"It's totally a word."

I chewed on the thought. "Fifteen thousand per day split or…"

"Per mermaid." Amelia's smile could have powered the city for a year.

"Sweet mother of pearl," I swore like a mermaid as I looked at the exchange rate. "I could be ready for a house by July if I can save all that."

"A house?" Amelia suddenly sounded sad. "You're getting a house?"

"That's the plan," I reminded her. "I've been working on my accounting degree and I'll finish classes in May."

"Americans have such a weird school schedule."

"Hush, you! That's not the point. And it's an Aussie school anyway." I turned in my seat so I could watch her expressions. "Listen, what matters is I can retire my fins after the winter cruise and move on with my life!"

"Move on?" Now she sounded horrified. "I thought you liked being a mermaid!"

"I do! It's good pay! But I want a job where everyone isn't paying to stare at my tits. It's so creepy having all the dads bring their kids to see me while their eyes never go above my neck. I want more than that. I want to be more than pretty. If someone loves me, I want it to be because they know me."

Amelia patted my leg. "I love you. Not like get-married-and-have-kids, but you are my best friend forever."

I patted her hand back. "I love you too, bestie."

"So, when you get this house and leave the mermaid life, are we still going to be besties?" Amelia's voice was serious.

Smiling I said, "Yup! Besties forever!"

"Cheers! Now let's go be mermaids and make that money!"

Three days of playing mermaid for a kid, and I'd be ready for the life I'd been dreaming about since I was in

Kindy.[13] I was going to have the job, the house, the perfect life.

I took a deep breath, trying hard not to get too excited or picture who would live that perfect life with me. But there would be someone. Someone with a loving smile all for me, who knew me and loved me all the same.

This was going to be the best Christmas break ever!

---

[13] Kindergarten, but Aussie-ified.

AMELIA STOPPED THE CAR TO ENTER A GATE CODE AT A BLACK, wrought-iron gate twisted to look like lily pads and flowers. Beyond the gate was a wide, winding road lined with flowering trees and bushes spaced so mansions played peek-a-boo with the drivers.

The riot of summer colors, all the greens and pinks and plums, made my fists itch just a little.

Huge, billion-dollar homes framed by carefully tended landscapes like jewels, while only a few miles away[14] there were people living twelve to a two-bedroom apartment because they couldn't afford anything better.

These people in their mansions had spent their whole lives swimming in money, while I'd spent every day I could remember trying to earn enough to eat.

Fifteen thousand a day.

A. DAY.

That was pure nonsense. Madder than a possum with a cut tail.

"Fifteen thousand," I whispered to myself. Who could afford that?

"Hmm? What?" Amelia asked, turning down the music she'd been blaring since we hit the highway.

I shook my head. "Nothing. Just talking to myself." Just hoping I wasn't getting myself in bed with the Australian mafia, or whatever they were called here. I wanted citizenship, dadgumit. I was building a new, better, beau-

---

[14] Sorry, kilometres.

tiful life and that could not include criminal elements in any way.

"Here we are." Amelia turned onto a driveway half hidden by large hedges covered in vibrant red flowers. "Fifty-seven-fifty-eight Mermaid Lane."

The view of the house opened in front of us. Pale stucco formed curving lines with red-tiled roofs that dipped into the flow of the trees and shrubbery almost like rocks in a coral reef.

Amelia drove along the side on a tiny paved lane that was more of a suggestion of a road than a real driving space, until we wound up driving into an equally tiny one-car garage nestled out of view of the main house.

"Here we are!" Amelia grinned at me. "I'll be back here tomorrow. No worries."

"Should I check in with the owners? Let them know I've arrived?"

"Sure." Amelia shrugged. "Drop your gear off first though." She held up an old-fashioned house key.

I shook my head in bewilderment. "Who uses keys these days?"

"We do, shipboard. Look, it's no worries, love. There's a couple of mermaid tails there and you'll be fine."

Taking the keys, I got out of the car and grabbed my suitcase from the back. "Anything else? Any warnings? Some greasy uncle to avoid or anything like that?"

Amelia shook her head. "Nah. Should be a good time. Hey, one more thing—"

I looked at her.

"Can you take the green box with you? I don't need it tonight."

"Sure." I put the small box on my luggage. "You will be here tomorrow, right? You're not abandoning me?"

"I'll be here! No worries!" She waved as I closed the door and she sped off.

Right.

So… vacation was going to start with three extra days of work. Not the original plan, but no big deal.

I wrinkled my nose. I didn't love surprise changes to my schedule. But then I reminded myself that three days of work were going to get me a down payment on a house. With a house I could start building my dream life. The one where I could decorate how I wanted. Paint the walls. Have more than ten outfits in something other than a tiny closet. Have a loving spouse who was excited to see me every day.

If I closed my eyes, I could picture everything, right down to the white picket fence and a toddler running in the grass to hug Daddy.

In my imagination *Daddy* had rich brown hair, and ocean blue flecks in his hungry brown eyes. I smacked myself in the forehead, trying to put Marcus Dupre well out of my thoughts.

The man lived on another continent.

I was about as likely to see him again as I was to find real mermaids at the beach.

With a sigh I forged ahead, finding a path of large white stones that led through more flowering side gardens and under some lillypilly trees toward the house's expansive backyard. I could already hear the rush of a waterfall and the lapping of pool water.

I looked down at the house key with suspicion. Shipboard we had keys for if we ever lost power or did a lockdown. Houses rarely had those issues. Unless you were poor.

We'd had keys for the trailer homes I'd grown up in.

While my classmates had keypads and homes with an ever-growing array of tech, I had keys and a hand-me-down gaming system that had been new sometime in the past century.

My father was a cruel, abusive man, but not stupid. He'd cottoned onto the fact that police and feds could track electronics in the home, so there was never an AI vacuum bot or a home system that turned on the TV with a voice command.

Even our cars were the old-fashioned kind with no Bluetooth connection or GPS. Nothing that could be used by anyone wanting to know where my family had been.

I'd never told Amelia, or anyone else at work, that. My new friends believed I'd grown up without a family, escaped the foster care system at eighteen, worked my way through college, and only come to Australia on a whim.

The reality of what I'd done to escape—from changing my name to abandoning every contact from my past—wouldn't make sense to someone like Amelia. She came from a doting, sprawling family who adored her no matter what she did. I said we were besties, but the truth was there wasn't anyone in my new life who knew about my old one. My past was a secret buried at the bottom of the ocean right next to Davey Jones's locker.

And, really, the physical key shouldn't have mattered, but it still felt like a bad omen.

"It doesn't matter," I told myself quietly. "Three days of this, and you can go buy your own home with whatever kind of key you want."

I came to a stop under a trio of giant jacarandas in front of a bright blue door attached to a cozy—well, I would have called it cabana, except it had all the walls and a tiled roof.

Granted, one of the walls was a set of clear glass doors that looked out over a swimming pool which connected to the rest of the property by flowing under the bridge I'd crossed and, presumably, off to the waterfall I could hear in the distance. It was a decent-sized pool too. Although I was probably biased, given I spent most of my swimming hours in a tiny mermaid tank.

A bright yellow couch meant to weather all weather sat on the small patio overlooking the pool. There was a set of shelves with stone tableware tucked to the side with a small sink and a cupboard that was likely hiding a small fridge.

It was smaller than I was certain the main house was, but there was a little living area with couches and a TV overlooking the glass wall, a decent-sized galley kitchen, and two bedrooms with a small bathroom in between.

One bedroom was decorated with soft jungle greens and pictures of parrots mid-flight. The other was a pale, summery blue with pictures of seashells in the waves. I dropped my gear there and put my yellow suitcase on the bed to unpack. Four pairs of clothes, two light dresses, a couple pairs of swim sets so I could keep the legendary Australian sun at bay while catching waves, and three pairs of shoes.

I tossed Amelia's box into the closet. Whatever it was, I didn't want to be involved. I hadn't gotten involved with my family's smuggling, and I was not getting involved now that I was free of them. Amelia's bad choices were entirely her own.

After I unpacked my clothes I went back to the bathroom, where six mermaid tails hung up.

They were all the newer silicone models. One was a fantastical, shimmery rainbow, two were very generic blues. There was a yellow tail with red streaks on the side, and the other two were pink and white. I picked the white tail with soft pink tips and spread my hands across the waist to do a guesstimate measure. I could work with this.

Magnolia the Southern Belle Mermaid.

Already the backstory for the character was forming in my mind. Enchanted moonlight, lost love, and forbidden kisses... Or, since this was a party for a kid, enchanted moonlight, lost gems, and a race to unlock the secrets of the deep ocean.

Yeah, that would work. Adventure, magic, and mystery were always a good story.

With a smile I embraced my inner mermaid, ready for as much adventure as a little kid's party and mysteriously flavored birthday cake could offer.

Sunbeams danced across the bottom of the azure-blue pool as I swam, absorbing a precious moment of silence. I surfaced with a smile to the hundred decibels of six little mermaid-obsessed five- and six-year-olds swimming in the pool like *real* live mermaids in *real* fabric mermaid tails.

Robyn, the blue-eyed birthday girl, was almost in tears she was so excited. The sparkly purple tail seemed to be everything she'd ever wanted.

"Miss Magnolia! Miss Magnolia!" She waved at me from the pool steps. "Watch me swim!" Pushing off, she glided through the water, little tail waving amazingly well for a beginner.

"Why, I do declare! It's almost as if you were born a mermaid!" I said in my silliest Southern Belle voice. "Are you sure you weren't born when a magnolia blossom fell in the water under a full moon like me?"

Robyn covered her mouth as she giggled, hiding where a missing tooth was. Six years old today, on summer break, and spoiled rotten by the most doting parents I'd seen in years. To get any more spoiled she'd have to be born a Dupre in New Orleans.

"Mommy! Mommy!" Robyn waved and dove under the water to swim to the pool edge.

Her mother, Madeleine, was sipping a bright pink drink and staying as far from the splash zone as possible while still trying to be present. She had honey-blonde hair, the same blue eyes as her daughter, and the golden tan of someone who was out in the sun plenty but who remembered her sunscreen.

I waved to another little girl in a blue tail who was jumping along the bottom of the pool rather than swimming. "Are you good?"

The little mermaid nodded eagerly and dived under the water, holding her nose and squinching her eyes shut.

All around me, little mermaids squealed in delight as I tried very hard not to think about the time. Theoretically, I was fine. I was used to doing four-hours shifts, but that usually involved less than an hour of swimming and lots of smiling and posing for pictures. Chasing kids in the water and swimming the whole time was a workout.

"Isla!" a voice rang out from the house with very parent-y tone.

I saw Madeleine's shoulders relax as a real smile returned to her face. "Isla! Your mummy is here! Let's get changed and get our party bags to go! LJ," she continued, risking a step closer to the water, "can you stay here and watch the pool while I say goodbye to people? I'll make sure to save some food for you."

"If you get food ready, shell yeah!" I smiled back at her. "I'll stay here with all the little mermaids and make sure they're safe."

A red-haired mini-mermaid swam up beside us. "Is *'shell yeah'* a bad word? I can't use bad words. I have a baby brother." Her green eyes were huge and solemn.

"Um..." I looked at Madeleine, mildly panicked. "Around little brothers you might say *'roll tide'* instead[15]."

---

[15] Look, I'd said it sarcastically once when I first got to the cruise ship and the Aussies were either A) having a go at me or B) honestly didn't know about the Crimson Tide, Roll Tide, or college football in the USA. At this point I was afraid to ask.

Madeleine nodded, her expression equally solemn. "Rolling tides are very good. In the far away magic magnolia oceans where Mermaid Magnolia comes from, it's a very common way to say you're happy."

"Roll tide!!!" the tiny red-head screamed. As long as she never went to Georgia[16] she'd be fine.

Madeleine waved at me and hurried inside to greet the arriving parents.

I swam a couple of loops around the pool, posing for pictures with the party goers as their families came to pick them up and waving goodbye until only Robyn and I were left at the pool.

She sat there, pale cheeks turning pink from the sun and loose blonde curls all tangled from swimming, running her hands over the tail.

"What's wrong, my little pearl?" I asked, swimming over to the steps to sit by her. "Sad your friends went home?"

"No." She sighed and looked back at the house. "Maybe?"

"I'm sure you'll see them again soon."

She nodded, not looking any happier. "Do I have to give up the tail?"

"No." I shook my head. Her mom had made it very clear the tails were presents for each of the girls. "This tail is yours forever and for always. Look how well it fits! Who else could it belong to?"

Robyn's bottom lip quivered. Big, fat tears pooled in her eyes. "What happens when I get big?" Robyn asked, her voice quavering.

I stared at her. Most kids did not think much further than next week, or to their next ice cream cone. "What do you mean?"

---

[16] Or Louisiana. Or Mississippi. Or Tennessee. Or... Well, basically anywhere in the Southeast United States that wasn't Auburn. They had a lot of rivals.

"What about when I'm mom-sized?" Robyn asked. "My tail will be too little! I won't be a real mermaid!" Full-on sobbing, Robyn turned to me, reaching for a hug.

There was no one else around. My mild panic became real.

Rule One at work was Do Not Touch Kids. I was a mermaid. I blew bubbles, waved, and splashed people with my tail. I didn't hug anyone.

One, it wasn't safe for the kids. Two, it wasn't safe for the people like me who didn't want an irate parent demanding I get fired as they sued the cruise company into bankruptcy.

But Robyn's mom was greeting someone in the front of the house and it seemed everyone else had gone to see the new arrival too.

Robyn looked up at me with tear-filled eyes.

I slid into the water and held out one of the little pink pool floaties for her to grab onto. "It's a mermaid tail, isn't it?"

She grabbed the floatie and nodded.

"So it's magical, isn't it?"

Squinting at her tail under the water she said, "Is it?"

"Mermaids are magical, aren't they?"

Robyn considered this as I swung us in slow, calming circles in the middle of the pool. "Maybe?"

"Maybe they're magical?" I asked as I made an exaggerated surprised face. "They can breathe under water. That sounds pretty magical to me. I can only usually do that with a SCUBA tank."

"Fish breath in the water and they're not magical," she countered.

I nodded in agreement. "Mermaids can change from fins to legs though, right? That's magical."

"Caterpillars can grow wings and become butterflies," Robyn said with a challenging glare that was heartbreakingly adorable.

Very valiantly, I didn't laugh. I nodded in solemn agreement as I thought of a counterpoint. "I think butterflies might be a little magical."

"Really?" Robyn's skeptical look was award-worthy. "Because tadpoles change to frogs, and that's not magic."

"Maybe it is," I said. "Maybe everything's a little bit magic."

Robyn's lip quivered as more tears appeared. "Not me! I'm not magical at all! I'm just boring!"

Gulping in a sob, she pushed away from the floatie and swam to the steps.

"I'm so ordinary! I'll never be—"

"Robyn!" A deep voice full of adoration and true Southern warmth came from the house.

Robyn gulped back a sob, rubbed her arm across her slimy nose, and turned. "Uncle Marcus?"

I narrowed my eyes at the figure striding out of the house. The sunlight behind him put him in shadow, but what a fine shadow he was. Broad shoulders, tapered waist, muscle definition even in a t-shirt and slacks.

He, and he was definitely a he, looked like he'd either just stepped out of a business meeting or off the plane while flying first class.

"Robyn! There's the most beautiful birthday girl in the world! How's my favorite princess, cher?"

Swimming into the shade of a jacaranda tree, I could see the man perfectly: six four, shoulders like a linebacker, cut muscles, chocolate-brown eyes with hints of ocean blue, sun-tanned skin, and rich brown hair that looked no different than the last time I saw him three years ago. Marcus "Mako" Dupre, prince of St. Tammany Parish.

He lifted Robyn out of the water like she weighed no more than a flower petal. Then lifted his eyes so they met mine. Ocean blue sparks in rich brown eyes. Ever changing. Ever shifting. Ever flirting.

"Hello, cher." His grin promised all kinds of wicked fun.

"Hello!" I said with a nice Canberra accent I'd picked up from Amelia. "You must be the uncle our girl's been going on about all arvo."[17]

"Has she now?" The Cajun accent faded just a little.

Weird.

Robyn shook her head. "I didn't say anything!" She punched her uncle's arm. "You said you weren't coming!"

"Ah, now, I wasn't going to, but something with work changed so I got to come. Aren't you happy? It's a fun surprise."

He smiled at Robyn but his eyes kept coming back to me. "Who's your friend, jellybean?"

"That's Miss Magnolia from New Orleans," Robyn announced proudly. Her eyes went wide. "Wait! That's where you live, Uncle Marcus! Do you know each other?"

Marcus Dupre's eyes had a terrifying glint. "Maybe we do, cher. Maybe we do."

All at once I could see my past life on a collision course with my perfect future.

I was, as a mermaid might say, totally and royally mucked.

---

[17] Afternoon, remember.

Escaping from Marcus was a matter of luck more than anything else. Robyn's family wanted to chat with him, and as soon as his attention was gone, so was I. The guest house was tucked away at the back of the property where he had no reason to wander. So I was safe. Ish.

A few hours later, after a good shower and washing off my borrowed tail, the sun was going down. I'd found some nibbles in the fridge, and the muscles in my neck were finally unknotting.

Sitting on my bed looking at my yellow suitcase, I contemplated the dangers of staying. Leaving meant giving up a lot of money. A HUGE amount.

It would mean giving up my hopes of having a house in the next year.

The cruise ship wasn't bad. No one harassed me. I had plenty of food. There were always new places to explore, but it also meant sharing a room and never collecting anything.

What I wanted—even though I wouldn't admit it out loud even at gunpoint—was a real home.

I wanted to come *home* at night.

To a place I decorated. To a place where I was safe. To a place where I felt loved for who I was, and not just for my perky tits or swishy mermaid tail.

"Ugh!" I kicked a decorative pillow, wishing Marcus would spontaneously combust and burn all my problems to ash when he did. If he told Amelia even half of what my family did, she'd never talk to me again.

Worse, she'd probably tell everyone on the crew. Once it filtered out to immigration, I was food for the sharks. One look at my family history and I wouldn't be qualified for anything but a one-way ticket back to the US of A.

Thunder rolled outside, echoing my mood.

I lay in the bed, thumbing through various social media accounts.

Amelia's face appeared, taking over the screen as her ringtone played.

"Hello?" I said, as I turned the phone on and sat up.

"LJ!" There was a crash in the background. "How are things?"

"Good," I said. "Where are you?"

Something loud clanged on Amelia's end. "Look, I was hoping to come meet you tonight, but there's something wrong with my car."

"Oh? Do you need me to come get you?"

"With what?" Amelia asked.

My face flushed with heat as I remembered our debates over me not buying a car. I wanted a good, used one, but not until I was actually on land regularly. "Sorry."

"No worries! How did the party go?"

"Fine." I pulled my knees to my chest. "The birthday girl seemed a little upset about her tail not growing with her, but otherwise it was good. No one told me about what we're doing tomorrow though. Are you sure this is a three-day gig?"

"I thin..."—another clattering sound—"I think it's pictures?" Amelia sounded like she was guessing. "My car should be good to go by ten and I'll meet you around eleven. Okay?"

I nodded even though she couldn't see me. "Sounds good."

There was another loud rattling sound from her end.

"You sure you're okay?"

"Yup. No worries! Talk to you soon!" Amelia hung up before I could argue more.

It wasn't my problem, it really wasn't.

If I told myself that enough times maybe I'd believe it.

White light flashed through the room, followed by a boom that shook the tiny guesthouse like I was still at sea.

The lights died.

An eerie silence stole the space, smothering the usual, comforting sounds of civilization. The AC, the fridge, the TV... all of them were quiet as the dead.

Then something hit the roof. Something big.

I scrambled to sit up, flipping my phone around so I could use the dim light to see better. It was nothing. It was probably nothing.

The roof overhead creaked and a sinking sense of dread pulled me down.

Turning on my phone's flashlight, I scrambled out of bed and checked the room next to me. There was a big jacaranda tree outside the window, but that tree, what I could see of it through the driving rain, was fine. I checked the living area next. The pool outside was churning like a whirlpool, but the windows were intact. All the electronics were dark, as expected, but the fridge would probably stay chilled for a few hours. It wasn't like I had any food in there anyway.

Behind me I heard a creak. The spine-chilling creak of broken wood and sagging plaster.

"Oh. Oh no." Turning, I rushed back to my room where my backpack sat next to the dresser. Open. With all my clothes in it.

I arrived in time to see the ceiling collapse into the open bag under a waterfall of filthy water.

"LJ?" Madeleine's voice rang out from the front door and a light swept the room. She must have run outside as soon as she heard the crash. "LJ? Are you all right?"

"I'm fine," I called out. "The roof... isn't."

She came in wearing a black tank top plastered to her skin by rain and a pair of matching silk shorts.

"Sorry to pull you out of bed?" I braced for rage.

"Sorry?" Her eyebrows went up. "My roof collapses and nearly kills you, and you're apologizing? LJ, I'm the one who's supposed to apologize." She shook her head. "That tree needed to be trimmed last winter. I knew it did. It just hasn't been a priority."

"Well, it's handled now." I forced myself to smile because I didn't know what else to do. No car. No clothes. No place to go.

Madeleine patted my arm as water started to swirl around my bare feet. "Are your things okay?"

"That's my bag." I shone my cellphone light on my backpack. "All of it except for what I'm wearing."

"Oh!" She walked through the sloshing water and picked it up. "Oh, frogs and fiddlesticks! I'm so sorry, LJ. Come on up to the house. I'll find you something to wear tonight."

I was already shaking my head. "No. It's quite all right. You've paid me plenty. I'll call a cab or something. Get a hotel room for the night."

"Oh! Please no!" She sounded genuinely upset by the idea. "I need you here tomorrow."

"I can come back in the morning. Besides, if it's raining we won—"

"Please?" Madeleine's eyes were wide with worry. "I'm going to make mermaid pancakes tomorrow. It would be so wonderful if you could sit with Robyn at breakfast. Eat with her. Talk with her. Please? Robyn needs this."

The roof creaked.

"Come on," Madeleine said, holding her phone and my soaked backpack in one hand and shooing me forward with the other. "We need to get out of here, then we can argue. There might be umbrellas by the front closet if you don't want to get wet."

"I just got out of the shower, a little rain—" I was going to say a little rain wouldn't hurt, but the front door slammed into the wall when I opened it. "The rain is going sideways."

We had gales like this at home. Full, proper hurricanes where the wind was screaming past at over a hundred knots and grass could stab through a tree trunk. This probably wasn't that bad. Probably. But dashing up the slippery stone path to the main house, the rain felt like a thousand tiny daggers.

Madeleine surged ahead of me, getting to the sliding glass door between the lounge area and the pool deck so she could open it.

The rain swept in ahead of us, and it took us both to slide the door closed again.

"Phew!" Madeleine smiled brightly at me. "Bit of a blow. Sorry!"

"I doubt it was your fault."

She shrugged. "Old habit."

"Maddy?" A man's voice echoed through the two-story living area from the balcony above. "Is everything okay?"

"Remember the old tree near the jacarandas we were debating getting trimmed?"

"The old Moreton Bay fig?"

"That'd be the one," Madeleine's smile never faltered. "We should have trimmed it."

There was a groan from upstairs. "How bad is it?"

"It took out the roof, along with the electricity, and the guesthouse is flooding. We can call insurance in the morning, but Miss LJ's clothes are all soaked. The ceiling collapsed in her room, on her stuff." Madeleine walked as she talked, putting my storm-ruined belongings in the huge sink in their laundry room. "I'm going to offer her the guest room upstairs, and some extra clothes."

"Sounds good," the man said. "LJ, sorry about the roof and your gear. We'll get it sorted out in the morning."

"Love," Madeleine said, "can you go make sure there's clean sheets in the guest room? The girls were playing up there earlier."

"Sure thing." He faded, another shadow in the gloom.

I shook my head. "It's very nice of you to offer this, but I'm the hired help. I can sleep on the couch. Or call a car and go to a hotel."

"You already said that," Madeleine said as the lights flickered. The light over the kitchen stove turned on. "And I already said I'd rather you stay. Is our house that scary? I promise, there's no big trees hanging over the roof here."

"I just don't want to be an imposition," I said.

Rolling her eyes, Madeleine walked to the cupboard in the laundry room and pulled out a pale blue towel that she held out like a peace offering. "I really, really want you here tomorrow. It's important to Robyn."

"I'll come back," I promised as I took the towel. "I just don't want to intrude on your family."

Or risk seeing Marcus again.

I had avoided the main house since the party ended and, for all I knew, he was still hanging around. Although I was probably safe if the guest room was free. Still... "Doesn't it ruin some of the magic if she sees me out of my mermaid costume?"

"No! That's what I want!" Madeleine insisted.

"You want to ruin the magic?" I couldn't keep the doubt out of my voice.

Madeleine shook her head as she took a towel for herself and sat down on the white tile of the living room. "I want Robyn to see that being a mermaid isn't the only thing that matters."

"Um..." I sat down across from her, drying my hair.

"I was obsessed with mermaids when I was little," Madeleine said. "OB. SESSED. It's all I ever talked about. It's all I thought about. All my books were about mermaids. I had stuffed mermaid dolls, and plastic ones, and mermaid posters.

"Then, one day when I was ten, I came home from school and all my mermaids were gone. All my books. All my posters. All my dolls. My mermaid t-shirts and my mermaid pens in my desk." Her ever-ready smile drooped. "All gone."

"Why?" I had a sinking feeling I knew.

She shrugged with a sad look on her face. "My mother told me it was time to stop chasing silly fantasies and grow up."

"Yeah." I nodded as I grimaced in sympathy. "I've heard that one before." From absolutely terrible parents who wanted to beat the childlike wonder out of their children.

"Mum's a professor of logic and mathematics in Victoria. My obsession with mermaids..." Madeleine sighed as she pushed her towel away. "My mother thought it was keeping me from growing up. So she banned all the silliness. All the illogical things. Instead of swim lessons, I had math club. Instead of mermaid art, she put up posters of famous buildings and trigonometry equations."

"Because everyone loves those?"

Another shrug. "Some people do. I didn't. Not at first, but I learned to. Year by year, I learned to keep my mouth shut and toe the line. I made sure my grades were high, that my teachers praised me, that everything I did fit my mother's desire for the practical."

"Sounds dreary."

"It was," Madeleine confessed. "But it got me through school! Got me into law school. Got me into a very good law firm here in Sydney. I had an apartment in Residences Two, the fancy tower apartments near Sydney Harbor. Everything was exactly what my mother wanted. Until I saw a street artist selling mermaid paintings for ten dollars." Her face softened into a smile. "I bought it on a whim. Then hid it in my closet for months because I didn't dare hang it up. I was so worried about what my mother wanted. About what she'd say if I broke her rules."

"So you got rid of it?" I guessed.

Madeleine shook her head as an impish smile appeared. "It's hanging upstairs in the hall. In the apartment I hung it up where it was the first thing anyone saw when they walked in." A dimple winked at me as she smiled. "That's the thing I realized back then: this is my life, not my mother's.

"I loved mermaids because I loved the sea, and the idea of living there, and, when I was little, I was convinced I saw a mermaid when I was swimming one day," Madeleine said. "Loving mermaids doesn't make me a bad adult. Or illogical. Or silly. It means I have something I love, and there's nothing wrong with that.

"Right now, Robyn loves mermaids. I want to let her have that. I want her to love mermaids, and the ocean, and exploring her world. But I want her to see that the tail isn't the only thing that makes a mermaid special.

"That's why I need you here tomorrow. I want Robyn to see you eating breakfast. Little, mermaid-shaped pancakes that I've been practicing making for weeks. I want her to talk to you about your shows, and your life outside the cruise lines. I want her to see that what makes you special isn't only the sparkly tail you sometimes wear."

"I'm not really that special," I said, cheeks burning in embarrassment as I looked down.

"Everyone's special," Madeleine insisted. "Besides, you change when you're a mermaid, don't you? You put on wigs and makeup. I think she needs to see that too. To understand that she can choose who she wants to be. She doesn't need to wait for a tail to magically appear, she can put one on. She doesn't need to wish her hair blue, she can dye it or wear a wig. She can be anything. She needs to know that."

"All right." I shrugged. "I'll stay here and be your mermaid, I guess."

Madeleine reached over and squeezed my hand. "Thank you. This means the world to me."

"Maddy?" Her husband's voice came down the stairs. "When did you do laundry last?"

Madeleine's eyes went wide. She gave my hand another squeeze then hurried to stand up. "Give me a minute. I was supposed to wash clothes last night, but with making the cake and cleaning the downstairs I forgot. I'm sure I have something. Your room is upstairs, second door on the right."

I took the stairs two at a time and went right, along the balcony overlooking the living area to a room that would be over the kitchen. There was a bathroom in the center of the hall and another flight of stairs going up to the third-floor loft that was either an office or play room. From outside I'd seen a telescope up there, but it might have been for show. Next to my room was a closet, open and sporting an array of amenities for guests like small shampoo bottles, slippers, and more towels.

Grabbing a towel, I gently pushed the door open and tried turning on the light. Nothing happened.

Either the kitchen light downstairs was on a generator, or it was one of the fancy ones with its own emergency solar panel backup. Either way, I was in the dark up here with only the lightning show outside lighting my way.

The room smelled of wild sage and citrus laundry soap. As my eyes adjusted to the shadows, I could see the bed tucked up under the window overlooking the pool, the fallen tree, and the coastline in the distance. I closed the window curtains, stripped off my soaking pajamas, dried off, and then realized I didn't have any other clothes to put on.

There was a knock at the door.

Wrapping my towel around me, I opened the door, expecting Madeleine—and found myself staring at Marcus as fire flickered between us.

He held up a small hurricane lamp, complete with oil and the tiny flame. In his other hand was a set of gray clothes. His lips quirked up to one side in a smile, but his eyes stayed on mine. "Having a fun night?"

"Hardly."

His grin widened. "I brought you some clothes, if you want them."

"Thank you." I took the soft cotton t-shirt and a pair of sweats that carried the familiar scent of dark chocolate and quiet mornings on the bayou.

"Do you want a lamp too?" He offered me the one he was holding. "I have another in my bedroom."

"Yes, thank you." Tossing the clothes behind me on the bed, I took the lamp gingerly. "Anything else?"

"The water's working, if you want a shower. Just be careful which door you go through, cher. The one on the left is mine." He winked and vanished into the darkness as thunder rumbled overhead.

My heart hammered in my chest. Like a little, tiny me deep inside was pounding on it, desperately trying to break out and grab something I couldn't even admit I wanted. It didn't matter how much I ignored the desperate inner voice begging me to pay attention: I knew I was going to dream of a beautiful future tonight, and Marcus was going to be in the middle of it whether I wanted him there or not.

Breakfast the next morning was pancakes. Mermaid pancakes with carefully poured, colored batter so the mermaids had pancake-gold hair, blue and purple tails, cute purple t-shirts, and a pink bow in their hair. It was mildly terrifying that Madeleine put that much artistic effort into pancakes. But Robyn was all smiles, so maybe it was worth it.

I sat next to Robyn at the counter dividing the kitchen from the casual living, rec room space that looked over the pool and answered questions about mermaid life.

"Where does your tail go?" the little girl demanded.

"The one I had last night is still in the guest house," I said. "Where's yours?"

"Upstairs in my bathroom."

I didn't dare ask how many bathrooms the house had. I already knew of at least five bedrooms, plus a formal living room and formal dining room downstairs and a movie room next to the garage. Having grown up sharing a bathroom with a family of five, it felt excessive. It probably wasn't, but it felt like it.

"How long can you hold your breath?" Robyn asked, casually beheading her pancake.

"About four minutes," I said. "My friend Amelia can hold hers for almost five, but she's been a mermaid longer than I have."

"But you don't actually breathe under water?"

"Nope."

"I thought mermaids could?" Robyn frowned at her mom.

Madeleine shrugged. "Not all mermaids are like that, dear. More pancakes?"

The door to the mud room on the far side of the rec room opened. "Maddy!"

"Luca!" Madeleine waved as her husband walked in wearing sandals, shorts, and a bright pink t-shirt with a mermaid sitting on a surfboard and the slogan *Ride The Best* over the logo for Sydney Surfboards. "Want a pancake?"

"Nah, I'm all good. The crew's here looking at the house. Miss LJ, I've got your tails out by the pool drying. Found this in the closet too. Wasn't one of ours so I thought it might be yours." He held out the green box Amelia had given me.

I took it from him with a smile. "Thanks. I'd forgotten about it. It's my bunkmate's."

"Bunkmate?" Robyn asked narrowing her eyes in six-year-old suspicion. "Is that your boyfriend?"

"Nah." I kept my smile firmly in place. "It's my roommate on board the cruise ship where I normally live."

"You live on a ship?"

"Yup! A big one! Most of the year I'm sailing around and being a mermaid in the cruise's mermaid show. I take lots of pictures. Wave to people. Blow heart-shaped bubbles under water."

Robyn's eyes went bright with excitement. "I want to do that!"

"You'll get to do that!" her mom said happily as she turned off the stove and put the last pancake on an unclaimed plate. "Today we're going to get your hair and makeup done, and go get photos at the beach with you in your mermaid tail!"

"Like Isla did?" Robyn was practically bouncing in her seat.

"Just like Isla did," Madeleine sounded smug. "You'll even have another mermaid with you! Miss LJ is going to come with to give you all the tips and tricks about being a fabulous, fin-tastic mermaid. Isn't that right LJ?"

"I sure will!" I beamed at the little girl as I wondered who the fin-flip Isla was and why it mattered so much.

Robyn pushed away her plate with the leftover pancake. "May I be excused?"

"How many pancakes did you eat?" her mother asked.

"Three!"

"Go. You're excused," her mom said.

Robyn dashed off, racing upstairs.

Once I was sure the little mermaid was well out of earshot, I turned back to Madeleine. "There is a tiny logistics problem with all of this. Most of my gear got ruined last night. I think my tail is probably okay, but I can't salvage any of my makeup. My wig is going to take at least a couple of days to fix. I don't even have casual clothes to wear to the photoshoot unless I wear these pajamas. I need to hit the shops. Problem is, I got dropped off by my friend Amelia. I don't have a car with me. Can I get a taxi out here?"

"Not to worry, cher," said a familiar voice that wrapped around me like a warm hug and threatened to strangle me like a snake wrapping around my throat.

I glanced up in time to see Marcus' smile as he put a couple of yellow, fabric shopping bags down.

He smiled. "Clothes. Swimming gear. Even found you some shoes."

"Oh!" Madeleine said, clearly distressed by the look of disgust on my face. "Please, please don't worry. Marcus is a cousin from the states, from my husband's side of the family. He had trouble sleeping, time zones and all that. So he volunteered to go shopping while I worked on breakfast." She held out the last plate of pancakes to Marcus.

Forcing a smile on my face for Madeleine and Robyn's sake, I nodded. "Perfect. Then, I have nothing slowing me down today. I'll go check the tails out by the pool and I'll be ready for this photoshoot adventure!"

"Perfect!" Madeleine clapped her hands together look-ing relieved.

Marcus cut off the tail of his mermaid pancake and winked at me.

I ignored him. It was that or lose my mind.

My life here in Australia relied on no one ever knowing about my past. People liked me because I was an average girl. I got along with people. I didn't rock the boat. I was calm, level-headed, and ready to try new things.

As soon as they realized I came from a family of crim-inals, my chance to build a new life was gone. I'd forever be the daughter of Jonny Pritchard. The stinking baby sister of Beau, Dawson, and Bobby.

I'd rather die than let that happen.

Which meant I needed to find a way to shut Marcus "Mako" Dupre up for good. How, I wasn't sure, but I'd think of something. In the meantime, I'd prep for a photo-shoot.

It took over an hour to sort things out, load my gear into several borrowed laundry baskets, and figure out my hair situation. Normally a wig made hairstyling easy and kept my look the same from show to show, but with the wig damaged, I had to style my own red hair and do every-thing possible to ensure it wouldn't go all over the place in the wind, waves, or whatever else arose.

By the time I was ready to load up the car, Robyn was squealing in excitement and their little car was packed. My stuff hadn't even made it into the trunk[18] and the car was full.

"Worried, cher?" Marcus' Cajun accent came from over my shoulder as the glitter of silver keys being tossed in the air flittered out of the corner of my eye.

---

[18] Or boot if you're an Aussie.

"No. Just wondering if I'm walking."

"We're taking two cars." Marcus nodded further down the drive to where a daisy-yellow car was parked. The license plate was completely normal, which meant it was either a rental or not Marcus' car. The man didn't do normal.

Madeleine popped up from ensuring Robyn was safely secured in her kiddy seat. "We're all set to go, and I'll make sure we have some lunch for this arvo. LJ, are you good to ride with Marcus?"

"Absolutely!" I lied with a smile. "I'm here to do my mermaid best to give Robyn a happy birthday!"

Marcus snickered but Madeleine beamed as if I were telling the truth.

I was in so much trouble.

Holding out a hand as he mockingly bowed, Marcus said, "M'lady's carriage awaits."

Since the rest of the family was in the other car, I rolled my eyes and walked past Marcus, tossing my gear in the back of the little yellow car as I did.

The car with Robyn's family rolled out and we followed, the radio playing some cutesy music about summertime beaches and Christmas kisses. Our little caravan of two left the neighborhood, merging onto the highway to drive south.

Every kilometer made me tenser and tenser. Marcus was being silent. Marcus, who couldn't even keep his mouth shut during tests in high school was be—

"So..."

There it was. In full Southern Drawl.

"So?" I asked, trying my best to keep my voice calm.

"You're alive," he said.

I nodded, ready for the blackmail. "Sure am."

"We all thought you were dead." There was a hint of anger in his tone and his accent was rougher. "Police figured you'd done run off the road and landed in a bayou.

Two other cars got run off that night by a drunk truck driver. All about the same time you left. But not until after the police called me in for questioning, thinking maybe I'd done something to you. I was the last one to see you."

His knuckles were white as he gripped the steering wheel.

"I didn't ask you to walk me out, or hit on me when I left," I said. "I got my pay. I left work. I didn't owe nobody nothing when I left."

Marcus' face twisted into an awful scowl.

"Did the police come the next day?"

His face softened a little into lines of regret. "No. When you didn't show up, Jenni decided you must not want the job. Threw a tantrum. Said you'd figure out right quick that no one else in the parish would hire a 'no good varmint' like you."

I snorted in amusement.

"Her words, not mine," he clarified.

"Doesn't matter." My accent was slipping into the familiar patterns of my old home to match Marcus' Creole drawl. "Everyone thought I was good for nothing, just like the rest of my no-good family."

"Yeah, well, it was that no-good papa of yours that blew it all out the water. He came into the bar a few weeks later demanding to know where you were."

I raised my eyebrows at that. "Why?"

"He'd near run out of beer money and the cable got switched off because the bills hadn't been paid."

"I left them with over a month's worth of money to pay the bills and buy the groceries." I knew when I did it that it probably wouldn't last.

Bobby would empty the account to buy drugs. Or my father would use it to buy alcohol. Or Beau and Dawson would lose it all gambling. But I'd left it all the same. So no one could ever say I stole from them.

Marcus glanced at me as we exited the highway, driving between eucalyptus trees toward the coast. "They're grown adults, Lainey Jane, they could take care of themselves if they wanted. No one's blaming you for wanting more."

"Liar." I crossed my arms. "I bet half the parish thought I'd done a runner. The rest were talking about how cruel I was to leave my daddy and my poor brothers all to themselves. Tongues were wagging about how I have no family loyalty. No care for others."

"There was some of that, yeah." He sighed. "Then someone said I'd been the last to talk to you. If there's anyone in the parish that can make tongues wag faster than your family, it's me. The Dupre's wild child.

"The parish police had all kinds of questions about that. What'd I do to you. Where'd I take you. I think they were wondering if they could lock me up, but one of my cousins found a security video from a truck parked on the side of the road that night showing you getting in your car and driving away. I went back in and wound up playing cards until dawn, so I was no longer a suspect."

"How nice," I said, trying to keep the edge of tension out of my voice. "What's it going to cost me to keep you from telling everyone about what happened?"

"Everyone back home you mean?" Marcus sounded honestly confused.

I rolled my eyes. "No, the people here. I've busted my tail to build myself a life here. I'm going to have Australian residency come February. I'm saving to buy a house and I'm working on a second degree, one in business and finance so I can work at a bank.

"If you come here and tell them about my family, about who I was before I was just LJ, I'm going to lose my job. I'll lose my chance at becoming an Aussie citizen. I lose everything I've been working on. So, I repeat: what's it going to cost me to shut you up?"

There was an unnatural silence in the car.

It was as if Marcus was holding his breath. Or maybe he'd died of shock.

I played with my purse strap like it was a fidget toy.

Marcus steered the car down the green, curving cliff-side toward a patch of beach where I could already see camera equipment set up in front of an azure-blue ocean.

The silence stretched like a winter night at the North Pole.

Finally Marcus took a steadying breath. "I didn't realize I was a villain in all this."

My snort of amusement was more one of disbelief. "You're Marcus 'Mako' Dupre. Your family has money and power in the parish. You can have anything and anyone you want. I turned you down, don't tell me that your ego wasn't bruised and you weren't planning a bit of revenge. Now you're a shark smelling blood in the water. Take your pound of flesh, all I'm asking is that you let me live."

"I offered you a ride that night because your car looked like it would fall apart if you sneezed! It had weeds growing on the windows!"

"That was on purpose! My brothers liked fancy cars. I took care of the engine and the innards, but I didn't wash it, so they didn't sell it."

We parked next to the beach.

"I'm not a monster," Marcus said. "I'm not"—he turned in his seat to look at me—"I'm not. Do you really think I'd hurt you? I'm happy you're alive! I'm happy you're over here living a good life! Why would I do anything to ruin that for you?"

"Because you can?"

His jaw dropped open as he stared past me to the beach as if the waves could give him answers. "Is that... Is that who you think I am? Someone who hurts people just because I can?"

I lifted a shoulder in a shrug. "Most men are. Look at my dad. Look at my brothers. Look at every man who ogled and harassed me when I worked the bar. Or who stares at my swim bra hoping it'll fall off and they'll get to see my tits while I swim as a mermaid. You flirt, you smile, and you expect to have my gratitude and then have access to my body."

"No!" His eyes met mine. "I flirted because I like you. You're smart, and funny, and caustic."

"Caustic?"

"Caustic." Marcus nodded, the corner of his mouth lifting in a seductive smile. "You're scathing, cher. Bitter and vicious as an angry gator." He lifted his shoulder in a shrug. "But, that's not a bad thing. Not everyone needs to be sweet little angels full of forgiveness and compassion. I'm not. We both know I'm not."

Crossing my arms, I snorted. "I guess."

Marcus shifted in his seat so he was facing me again. "I smile because I'm happy most of the time. My life is good. I have a good family, a good career, a good future. I never treated you like you owed me, did I?"

Taking a breath, I bit back my automatic retort and tried to remember a specific incidence. "That last night, at the bar, you said you dreamed about me. You told the men there I was your property."

"I had dreamed about you." Marcus' expression turned serious. "And I told them that because I meant you were under my protection. You were one of my people."

I stared at him using the icy gaze I'd learned to make drunks at the bar back off.

He looked down for a moment, then back at me, real regret in his eyes. "I'm sorry that I made it sound sexual, or even possessive. I meant that you had the protection of my family. You were my friend from school, and I would have helped you any time you asked."

"Have I ever asked for help?" I raised an eyebrow at him. "Am I that type of person?"

"Everyone should be that type of person," Marcus said with the most earnest expression I'd ever seen on his face. "Everyone needs help sometimes. Everyone needs love and support. Humans are social creatures. We swim with a pod, or run with a pack, or whatever group noun will make you happy."

He ran his hand through his dark hair as he sighed and looked out at the beach.

"Not everyone was born with a pod to swim with," I said, unlocking the car door, "or someone to turn to. And not everyone needs other people."

"Everyone needs someone they can count on." He said it as if it were part of an old argument, something he'd repeated to someone else more than once.

"Just give me your price, Marcus."

"Will you believe me if I say there is no price?"

"Not really."

With a sigh, he scowled out at the waves, refusing to look at me. Then lifted his shoulder in a shrug. "Fine. Pay me what you owe me from back then. The last thing you said to me was that I could buy you a drink next time I saw you. Let me buy you a drink, and I'll not tell a soul that Lainey Jane lives and breathes."

"Done." I got out of the car before he could add any other demands.

My stomach twisted in a tangled knot of bitter memories. Marcus was part of my old life. Part of the world where I'd suffered humiliation, hunger, and everything else. His memories of that time were different, and that was fine, he was allowed to be a dreamer.

But that didn't change anything.

For my new life to be successful, my old life had to stay dead and buried. Marcus could be as handsome as he wanted to be but he couldn't be part of my future. I had to survive alone or not at all. I couldn't take someone like Marcus—someone from my old life—and make them part of my new life.

More recent memories of Amelia and the rest of the crew helping me learn the ropes of the mermaid life pushed against the darker memories of my youth. There were good people in the world. There were good times and happy memories.

If I clung to that belief like a life raft maybe—just maybe—I'd find a way to build myself a better future.

"Mermaid Magnolia!" Robyn ran across the sand to me, frothy blonde wig with sparkles bouncing on her head.

"Mermaid Robyn!" I put on my best mermaid smile.

Whatever else happened, I wasn't going to be a scowling fraidy-fish on Robyn's big day. I was going to be all smiles, hope, and my very merry, mermaid best.

THE SUN WAS SINKING LOW IN THE SKY BY THE TIME ROBYN wiggled out of her tail and raced off across the golden sand.

I was still on a rock, trying to avoid getting cut by barnacles, and wondering how in the name of the tides I was going to get down. Ocean waves slapped the rock, splashing me with chill water. There was colder water in the world, to be sure, but the seventy degree waves were a far cry from a hot bath. After a few hours here I was starting to shiver.

The camera crew were gathered around Robyn, giving her all the attention, which she deserved. It just left me in a bit of pickle.

If I flopped forward I could probably get down without breaking anything, but there were other rocks down there, so getting cut was a strong possibility. If I waited for the tide to come in…

"Ça va, cher? Need some help getting down?"

"Only getting down gracefully."

Marcus stopped beside me, feet sinking into the wet sand as the water splashed his black swim trunks. His smile was amused, but not cruel. "Can I touch you?"

"Yes," I finally said with a huff of annoyance. "Help me get down, and I can hop across to the chairs." I reached for his steadying arm.

He scooped me up like I weighed nothing and carried me to the chairs in the dry sand.

I absolutely did not notice his arm muscles, or how warm he was, or even think about how easy it would be to sink into his embrace and relax for a moment.

None of those things even crossed my mind. Just because his voice was familiar and soothing, and the heat coming off his body could have melted a glacier, didn't mean I was falling for it. I was stronger than that.

Which is why I barely noticed the chill of the evening wind when he set my gently in the beach chair.

"Thank you."

"Any time, cher." His eyes twinkled with pure devilment.

Humphing in annoyance I turned my attention back to matters at hand.

"Need help taking off that tail?"

"No**p**e." I popped the P hard. "I can do this all by myself. I have a system."

"Doesn't mean it couldn't be more fun with a little," he paused for an infinitesimal moment, "hel**p**." He popped the P too, mimicking me perfectly, and chuckled.

I shot him a glare that had scared off many a wandering hand—and a small reef shark in the cruise ship's aquarium—to no avail.

Marcus' smile put the sun to shame.

In my head, swords clashed.

"What are your big plans, cher?"

"For life?" I asked as I started to roll my tail down.

His gaze miraculously stayed on my face despite the black bootie shorts being visible. "For dinner. I promised you one, no?"

The temptation to shrug it off and pick up Macca's[19] was there. A part of me really wanted this to just be over with. But, it was a free dinner. "What do you like?"

"You."

I rolled my eyes. "I meant to eat."

---

[19] McDonald's, for the non-Aussies in the crowd.

His smile turned wicked.

"For dinner."

"Cher…" He shook his head. "You need to stop making it so easy."

Pulling my tail off, I flapped it, sending sand spraying in his direction.

"What?" He laughed. "We're in the Down Under, are we not?"

"Shush! Robyn's headed this way." I gave him another quelling glare, but his smile was infectious. Sweet water and tides below, the man could corrupt a saint. One look at the sparkle in his eyes and I wanted in on whatever he was offering.

I knew better. Of course I knew better! Marcus Dupre was nothing but trouble.

"Magnolia!" Robyn rushed up to me and gave me a big hug. "This was the best day ever!"

"Thank you," Madeleine said, patting her daughter's shoulder as if to reassure herself the girl was still there. "Really this was fantastic. I feel I ought to pay you extra."

"No worries!" I waved my hand, brushing away the thought as I smiled. "I had a fin-tastic day with your little mermaid! She's going to be queen of the oceans some day!"

Madeleine ruffled her daughter's hair. "Maybe."

"Tough job, being queen," Marcus said. "Think you're up for it?"

Robyn nodded enthusiastically.

Madeleine and Marcus exchanged sympathetic looks. Clearly there was something going on there that I was missing. It wasn't a romantic vibe, but something. Almost heartbroken?

I waited until Madeleine and Robyn had said their goodbyes and gotten in the car before I turned to Marcus. "What was that look with Madeleine?"

"Which look?"

"The super sad look like someone was going to die? Is Robyn ill? Is it terminal? Was this some last wish type of thing?"

That would explain the expense, now that I thought about it.

Oh my fins and flippers!

I was such a monster.

I'd been hating on the family's obscene spending habits out of old jealousies and they were splurging to give their daughter her last moments of happiness.

Marcus shook his head. "Whatever you're thinkin', cher, don't. It's not like that."

"She's okay?" I reached for his arm but stopped short.

He sighed, his gaze drifting to the ocean as if the surf could take away his worries. "She's not growing... quite right." Looking at the sand he shoved a foot in, digging a little hole.

"How bad is it?" My fingers tangled around his sleeve in worry.

"Not fatal. But it makes her feel different."

"So the mermaid thing?"

"Makes her feel special. Like she belongs somewhere." He smiled up at me and that smile, genuine and kind, broke something in my heart. Marcus Dupre, despite his wild childhood, had grown up to be a decent man.

I let go and looked away, desperate to find an escape hatch for this conversation. Brushing sand off my leg, I gave Marcus my most cheerful stage smile, the one I used for every photo session with handsy customers. "Right. So. Showers are where? I need to rinse off."

"There's a public shower over there." Marcus nodded over his shoulder.

"Perfect. I'll go rinse off, we can take all this home, and then go fin—"

My phone rang with the bright notes of Mermaid Melody.[20]

"Hold on," I said. "That's Amelia's ringtone." Holding up a finger to forestall any further questions, I answered. "What's up?"

"LJ?" Amelia sounded breathless, and not the good kind of just-rolled-into-bed-with-a-hottie breathless; more like a stressed-and-about-to-cry breathless.

"Yeah. What's wrong?"

"Nothing." The lie was all over her voice. "No worries. You still have the box I gave to you?"

"Yeah."

"Great! Great. Can you come by the Darling-Est Bar by Darling Harbor. You know the one?"

A vague memory of a skeezy club turned pub with broken exercise bikes in the back corner and the rank smell of mildew in the loo mugged me. We'd gone there on our last shore leave on accident. Or, at least I thought it was on accident.

"LJ?" Amelia's voice cut through my memories.

I nodded even though she couldn't see me. "Yeah. The place we went to last time?"

"Yes!"

Maybe they'd cleaned it up since then. "Sure. I can be there in about an hour."

"Great! See ya soonest!"

I met Marcus' eyes as I hung up.

He raised an eyebrow in question.

"Want to grab dinner over by Darling Harbor?"

---

[20] From the kiddy cartoon *Melody Mermaid Sings A Sea Note.* I don't know where it comes from, but the twenty-minute episodes play 24 hours a day in the shipboard daycare and I've never seen a repeat episode. It's terrifying.

"Sure. Got a place in mind?"

"Yup. At least for the starters." If my shoes stuck to the floor again, we were eating somewhere else.

Sighing, I heaved my mermaid tail over my shoulder and marched off to rinse in the public showers. I was like a cursed Cinderella. Everything was going wrong and I owed people favors, but, by midnight, I'd be free.

AROUND THE TURN OF THE CENTURY, SYDNEY ONLY[21] HAD A population of four million. It had grown to almost double that in the past few decades and the demand for space along the waterfronts meant there was an odd mix of wide roads, green spaces, trendy restaurants, and tiny side alleys with backroom bars. By the time Marcus and I found parking it was dark and the whole street smelled of second-hand beer mixed with low tide.

I got out of the car and opened the door to a hand being held in front of my face. Looking up at Marcus, I tilted my head in question, but took his hand.

He smiled. "Hi. I'm Marcus Dupre."

"I know that." I took my hand back as I shut the door. "Why are you introducing yourself?"

"I thought we'd start over."

Raising an eyebrow in question, I frowned at him. "Start over?" Looking around at the crowds, I tried to mentally process that idea. "I've known you since fifth grade. It's been over fourteen years."

"Yeah, but, cher, I didn't make a good impression back then." He hit me with the full force of his Cajun smile, pure sin and the offer of very good sex.

I rolled my eyes and started walking.

It had been a long day, I was tired, I was hungry, and whatever Amelia was up to, I didn't like it. I liked having

____

21 I say ONLY because some of the other cities the cruise hit had populations well over twenty million.

Marcus along for the ride even less because it meant my Before and After were combining.

Marcus relented with a smile and a shrug, catching up to me in a few strides. "You say all the memories of me are bad ones. Why not let me help you make new memories?"

"Because I don't need new memories of you? I have a new life. I've moved on." The argument sounded hollow even to me.

With a sigh, I stopped, letting the evening crowd swirl around us with the smell of fried fish and old beer. "Why do you want this? I'm..." I took a deep breath and stared before shaking my head.

"Listen," I said. "I was born in Oklahoma."

"I thought you were born in Texas?"

"No, it was Oklahoma. In the panhandle. We moved when I was three." A cold, familiar dread seeped into my bones as I spoke. "My parents got work in Houston. Maybe it was legit? My mom was selling something. Houses, or cars, or who knows what. All I remember was she'd go to trade shows for long weekends and my dad would bring his girlfriends over. But she was there most weekdays. Until, one day, I got home and no one was there.

"My mom didn't come home.

"My dad's solution was to have Beau watch me. He'd been suspended for fighting at school, so I came home to my thirteen-year-old brother watching me. Then a neighbor. Then my family gave up and just set out a box of crackers for me to eat when I got home. Child services came once, but my dad bribed them or something. Then we ran to Louisiana when I was ten."

Marcus nodded. "Beau was in high school."

"Seventeen," I said, lost in the horror of the memories. "A junior. He dropped out over the summer. Dawson dropped out at sixteen. Bobby quit showing up before high school. I think my dad listed him as homeschooled, claimed he was doing some religious curriculum. But it was one he bought from a garage sale. All the workbooks were filled in, and all Bobby had to do was add his name. He managed it for about three days before he made me start signing for him. He had other things to do." Hotwiring cars. Selling drugs to the neighbors. Gambling.

Our Bobby did love his gambling. Just like Beau loved stretching out on the couch eating whatever was messiest as he watched whatever sport was in season. Beau did as he was told and thought whatever you'd told him to think last.

Bobby had a more mercurial temper. He was in a good mood when you gave him what he wanted and violent when you didn't.

Dawson, ever the middle child, was easy to forget. He was smart the same way my dad was, cunning in a crooked sort of way. He wanted big things, and the only reason he didn't have them is that my dad broke his arm last time Dawson tried to con him.

In my mind I could still picture all three: big, brawny boys who all looked like variants of our father. Greasy, dirty blond hair with a hint of our mom's red, a scattering of freckles and persistently red cheeks from sunburn. Beau was the biggest, built like a linebacker, and acted like he'd had one too many concussions. Dawson was leaner and meaner. Bobby was as thin as I was because half the drugs he did took his appetite away.

A little piece of me still had the childish wish that I could make them love me. That I could wave a magic wand, or speak some magic word, and make them love me the way I had loved my big brothers when I was a starry-eyed little girl.

But reality was reality.

No one had wanted me as a child. No one had loved me. They had used me. First as a tax write off. And then as unpaid labor. And then for my paycheck.

All I'd ever been to anyone was a means to an end.

I shoved all the memories away, praying they'd drown in the bay along with yesterday's trash.

Marcus looked at me with concern.

Shaking my head, I said, "All I ever was to anybody in that town was *'that Pritchard girl'*. No one bothered learning my name or my face. No one cared how I was doing as long as I shut up and did what they said. Why would I want to go back to that?"

"I'm not saying you should go back to it," Marcus said, almost quiet enough to miss. "I'm not saying you ought to come back home to Louisiana with me."

"You're not saying sorry either."

Dark brown eyes speckled by ocean blue bored into me. "I didn't know I needed to."

"That's the problem. No one ever does. No one ever stopped to apologize to me. No one ever stopped to take care of me. No one ever stopped my family. They all looked the other way and let them use me and abuse me, because it was none of their business. Or they didn't want trouble. Or my dad paid them to look the other way." I let out a huff of annoyance and tried to find my calm.

Marcus reached for my hand. "I'm sorry."

He sounded like he meant it. Which is why I looked away, not quite ready to deal with the inevitable storm of tears a real apology could bring.

All these years. *All these years* of pain.

Of being ignored. Shoved aside. Treated like the only thing that gave me value was how much work I could do for someone else.

That was something to unpack with my therapist next week. I didn't need to think about it here, on the dock, while looking out at the big, blue... Okay, ocean was the wrong word. And the water wasn't blue at night.

Still. I didn't need to think about it while looking out over the dark, scummy waters of a busy marina.

"Forget it. It's all in the past. I just—" Looking him up and down, I tried to shake it off.

"I'm sorry," Marcus offered.

I shook my head. "I thought I was over all of it. But having you here, having you be in my new life…" I shook my head. "I don't know how to make that work."

Patting my face so my mascara didn't smear, I checked my phone for Amelia's map and nodded to the left. "I'm just hungry and tired. Let's get Amelia and be done with tonight. This way."

I pushed past a gaggle of drunken tourists taking pictures in front of a poster with a kangaroo holding a chicken for reasons I couldn't quite fathom. "The bar is up here. It was a French restaurant the first time we came, then a nightclub that played French pop music, then whatever it was six months ago. Hopefully it's better now."

Not that I was really expecting it. This corner of Darling Harbor had looked worse every time I came by.

There'd been an economic boom in the area in the late 30's, followed by rapid build up and then a fabulous crash in the 40's when people realized that big cities required more work than the city officials were willing to invest. You could fit twenty million people into a city and make it work. Tokyo was a fabulously run city. Sydney struggled when it got over eight million. Something about having over a quarter of the country's population living in one place could do that.

Marcus' hand slipped into mine, warm and calloused, tugging me toward the wall and away from the busy foot traffic. "You sure you're okay, cher? Amelia can wait a little bit if you need time. We don't need to rush this."

For a fraction of a moment, I let myself have this.

I let myself pretend Marcus Dupre cared about me. I let myself pretend someone loved me.

It was fun, for a couple of seconds, and then reality hit like a two-by-four with rusty nails in it.

Extracting my hand from Marcus', I smiled at him with my best, showstopping, mermaid-a-rific smile. "Thank you for caring!"

His eyes narrowed. "That's your customer service voice."

"I'm doing fin-tastic!" My grin stretched and I was certain murder flared in my eyes. "Let's keep moving!"

"That was creepy." Marcus took a step back and looked reasonably intimidated. But, like the Dupre he was, it only lasted half a heartbeat before he caught up with me. "You're very scary when you're angry, cher."

I rolled my eyes.

He bumped my shoulder.

"If you tell me to smile I will throw you into the water." I liked to keep my emotions neatly sorted and tucked away. Airing them like fresh-washed laundry felt personal. Intimate, almost.

Marcus looked over my head at the harbor water, oblivious to my internal conflict. "That's filthy."

"Most ports are." The ship's crew had required medical checks after every port-of-call. I eyed the dark waters with suspicion. "Still, probably safer to swim in that than kiss anyone at these bars. Try not to catch anything you don't already have, will you?"

"Are you telling me not to kiss strangers under the mistletoe over there?" Marcus' grin was a wicked invitation to pure trouble.

"As a rule, you shouldn't kiss anyone without warning."

He saluted like I was a boat captain. "Understood. When I kiss you, I'll let you know what I plan to do."

I rolled my eyes and plunged into the crowd as I pulled up the picture Amelia had sent me. Her usually bright blue eyes were a little puffy and red, like she'd been crying, and her blonde hair was pulled back in a messy bun that gave

Grandma Vibes. Her bright yellow shirt was the one we wore in the Mermaid's Kids Cafe on the ship.

I texted Amelia: *I'm outside. Where are you?*

She didn't respond.

I tried calling, letting the ringer go to voicemail twice. Her phone was either dead or turned to silent. Time for the old-fashioned approach.

"We're looking for this," I told Marcus, showing him the picture. "Amelia is a couple of inches taller than me in flats, and usually has heels on. You take the right side. I'll take the left. If you see her, tell her you're LJ's friend."

"You know Amelia is Luca's cousin, right?"

"What?" I stared in confusion. "She's related to Madeleine's husband?"

Marcus nodded. "Yeah. You didn't know?"

I shook my head. "That explains the job though." Giving Marcus a push, I titled my chin to the far side of the bar. "Go look for her."

That little sea snake! When I got Amelia out of whatever mess she'd wandered into, we were going to have *words* about this. There was nothing wrong about getting a job with family, but I would have played it a bit different if I'd known. Name-dropped Amelia a little bit more. Built up the excitement about her coming to visit Robyn. Something that showed them I was one of them.

Wending my way through the crowd like a fish swimming upstream, I started looking for blondes. Somewhere in this mess was my roommate who needed the box I had and a rescue from whatever side hell-stle[22] she'd gotten herself into.

A tall man stumbled into me, smelling of skipped showers and beer. He glanced down; for an eerie moment, I thought I was looking at Beau's face. All red, and scruffy, with narrow hazel eyes and the sour smell of trouble.

---

[22] Like a side hustle but way worse.

It was enough to make me step back, blinking.

The man had turned already, shaking his head as he staggered away.

Pushing my way through the bar, I scanned the shadows, searching for Amelia. There was a gaggle of ladies out on a hen's night[23] with one of them wearing a crown of cocks.[24] At other tables I saw couples of all types, mostly young though. The bar was probably too new to have regulars.

What I didn't see was Amelia. Anywhere.

"Want a drink?"

I looked up, ready to say no, when I saw the men in front of me had moved and left me standing at the bar. "I'm the designated driver," I lied. "My friend called and told me to pick her up." Turning my screen on, I turned my phone to the bar keep. "Have you seen her?"

"Upstairs patio," he said with a nod to some narrow stairs I thought went to a storage room. "She's still on drink number one though."

"You can never be too safe," I said with a sunny smile I used when teaching mermaid swim lessons to little kids. "Thanks!"

"No worries." The bar keep nodded to the person behind me.

It took a minute or two to snake my way through the crowd, but I reached the stairs and scanned the faces, looking for Marcus. He was nowhere in sight. He probably hadn't left me. Or Amelia, really. She was the family member he was after. I was probably an afterthought.

Even as I thought the words I cringed a little. My inner critic was *loud* tonight. Always assuming the worst. Always picking up on the negative.

---

[23] A bachelorette party.
[24] The birds, not the other kind.

It didn't help that a lot of my early life the inner critic had been right. Things always seemed to go from Bad to Worse to Worst.

"But I flipped the script," I whispered to myself. "I got out. I moved on. I reinvented myself. I'm someone new, brave, happy, and lucky." With each word I took another step up into a narrow hall painted in black that did, to be fair to the barkeep, end with a door open onto a patio that looked like it was built on the roof of the neighboring building.

Hopefully it was built correctly. I'd heard stories about the rushed construction in downtown Sydney.

The upper patio had glittering red and green lights on the railing, with sun-faded, faux-pine wreaths hanging at various intervals. In amongst the dense crowd, round black tables were strewn with black chairs in a haphazard mess.

Another burly man brushed past me, talking on his phone. I thought I heard the word "Janey", the name my brothers used to call me.

I shook it off.

Music blared from the speakers. "*Gotta, gotta, gotta catch that girl!*" the singer bellowed in my ear.

"Run!" Marcus shouted from somewhere in the crowd.

Amelia appeared wearing a cute red dress, ducking around two men wearing loose gray shirts.

One of the men in gray fell down, and I saw Marcus on the other side of the crowd, fists up.

"Oh, this is fin-tastic." I grabbed Amelia's arm as she almost missed the door and went over the side rail. "This way."

"LJ?" Tear streaks stained both her cheeks. "Oh! I'm so flippin' glad I found you!" She tried to hug me as we stumbled down the steps.

"What happened?"

Amelia pushed me forward as we hit the main bar floor. "Hurry. Hurry!"

"Ameli—" Heavy bootsteps behind me on the stairs cut me off.

Taking Amelia's arm, I pulled her toward the front door.

A large-set man with no hair tumbled down the stairs.

"Run!" Marcus' order had all the fire of Cajun cooking. He grabbed Amelia's hand as he sped past and dashed out of the bar.

Cursing under my breath, I ran after them into the crowds and chaos of Sydney Harbor at night.

WHICH WAY HAD THEY GONE? ALL AROUND ME, THE MESS OF holiday partygoers swirled on the dock. Drunken ladies on a hen's night. A family out celebrating grandpa's birthday with matching t-shirts, cake, and two screaming infants. Bros laughing as they walked, talking about sports, and flirting with the drunken ladies.

Someone bumped into me—one of the men in the gray shirts. Probably one Marcus had punched too, based on the blood dripping from his nose.

Quiet as a coon, I slunk backward, trying to find the shadows so the angry men didn't notice me.

I'd survived bar fights before. I could do it again.

Marcus would go to the car, wouldn't he? That made the most sense. Get out. Get out of the area. Find an alibi. That's how you pulled off things like this without getting arrested.

The upper bar lounge—patio, whatever—had been crowded and poorly lit. Any cameras up there probably didn't have enough visibility to ID Marcus or Amelia. If they did, well, Marcus was a Dupre. Even in Australia he could probably buy himself out of any major trouble. The worst he'd deal with was getting his tourist visa revoked. Amelia would be in more trouble.

All because of the box I still had in my purse.

My stomach twisted with unease as I slipped along the edge of the evening crowd. They were getting rowdier, even with men running—

"That one!" someone shouted behind me.

Like everyone else, I turned to look.

The tall, bald man who'd fallen down the stairs was pointing at me.

"Duck this!" I swore in my default mermaid tone and ran. Where I was going didn't matter anymore. Forward was good. Through the crowds.

I dashed right, skipping through a gift shop and nearly knocking over a tray of mermaid dolls.

The far side of the wall was open to a little square with a fountain. I ran past a food truck selling something that smelled deliciously spicy, around another truck with fancy looking pastries, and nearly smacked my face on a brick wall.

Another turn and I was rushing down an alley into darkness.

The sounds of the dock faded.

The murmur of the crowds and the music from the restaurants all became quiet until all I could hear was my shoes slapping along the pavement. I slowed down, panting in the darkness.

What. The ever-lovin'. Duckin' bells. Had just happened? Patting my back pocket, I pulled out my phone. Someone had some explaining to do.

Footsteps echoed down the alley, bouncing off the dumpsters and locked back doors.

I turned my phone off, shoving it back in my pocket so the light wouldn't give me away.

Somewhere above us, someone opened a window so slowly strobing purple and blue lights melted along the upper walls of a stone building.

Shrinking in on myself, I glided backward as silently as I knew how. And I knew a lot about staying out of the way of angry men.

"Lainey Jane?" The alley warped the voice, making it sound odd and almost watery. "LJ?"

Light pierced the darkness as a door opened upstairs and fell on Marcus' face.

My shoulders slumped in relief. "I'm here." I stepped forward.

"LJ!" He ran to me. Grabbed my shoulders. Pulled me into a hug that smelled of bayous, and magnolias, and home.

Wrapping my arms around him, I let myself have a tiny, tiny moment of peace before I let reality swell around me.

With a shake of my head I stepped back. "Where's Amelia?"

"Bringing the car around." Marcus nodded toward a small side alley.

"How'd you know where I was?"

He shook his head, not quite out of breath but looking like he'd run his fastest sprint time ever. "Luck. I thought I saw you through some windows."

My mind tumbled over worst case scenarios. Terrible things like tracking devices in my purse or Marcus paying someone to scare me so he could play the hero. I'd learned as a child that trust wasn't something I could give to anyone. And yet... *And yet...*

I felt safe.

Before I could let myself overthink that emotion, I took another step away from Marcus.

He let me go without any comment and led the way to a small back door to some pub that was propped open. We skirted along the back halls, past the coat racks and the delivery pick-ups, out the front to where Amelia was waiting in Marcus' car.

I slid into the passenger seat as Marcus took the driver seat from Amelia. "Here's your box," I said, tossing it at her.

She caught it, then leaned far forward as possible with her seatbelt on. "Are you okay?"

"Yes." My jaw ached from not grinding my teeth. "Want to explain what's happening?"

"Um..."

I didn't even need to look into the mirror to know Amelia was blushing.

"You can start with explaining why the flip you didn't tell me I was going to spend three days with your family. That's one of those little details that would have helped to know."

There was a groan of dismay from the backseat and her shadow fell away as Marcus merged onto the highway.

"Spill," I ordered. "Before I gut you and toss you out like chum bait."

"I didn't mean for it to cause any strife," Amelia said with a weary sigh. "I just, I know you hate family time and all that. You never visit yours or talk about them. And I knew you grew up pretty poor. So I didn't want to rub it in. It seemed rude to ask you to come over to my cousin's big house and get paid by family. It's not a handout or anything. It's what my aunt offered. And she picked you from the roster."

"Possibly because you told Madeleine that LJ is the most honest of the mermaids and won't have the police knocking on her door?" Marcus' tone was grim.

Amelia huffed in annoyance. "You're so serious! Having fun doesn't make them bad people."

"Was that what tonight was?" Marcus asked. "Having fun?"

"No. Hold up!" Amelia leaned forward again. "You called LJ by some other name tonight, right? Do you know each other?"

"No," Marcus said as I reluctantly admitted, "Yes."

I glanced at him, met his eyes, and shook my head.

"No," I said as he said, "Yes."

Rolling my eyes I said, "Oh, for the love of mudpuppies. Yes! All right. Yes. I knew Marcus when I was younger. Before I moved to Australia."

"Remember a couple years back when the family was all worried because the police thought I'd murdered some local girl?" Marcus asked.

"Yeah," Amelia said.

"She's that local girl."

I could feel the weight of Amelia's stare.

"I left town without telling anyone," I admitted. "Some people got the wrong idea."

"It took them a couple of weeks to notice she was gone," Marcus said, as if that helped. "But once they realized, they wanted someone to blame."

"How were you the logical person?" Amelia sounded horrified, and confused. "You're the sweetest man on the planet! I've seen you try to save a cockroach!"

It was a good thing it was too dark out for them to see my expression. *Sweet* and *Marcus Dupre* were not words I ever imagined going together.

Although, now that I thought about it, I couldn't remember a time he'd been out and out cruel to anyone either. A ridiculous flirt with the attention span of a gnat, maybe. But no one seemed mad at him all that often. He had what the local grandmas called a "rapscallion's smile" and was too cute for his own good.

"I can hear you," Marcus said.

"What?" Amelia asked. "Of course you can hear me. I'm talking!"

"I meant Lainey Jane." Marcus took the highway turn off back to the house. "She's cussing me out in her head. Aren't you, cher?"

"I was doing no such thing." I crossed my arms. "And it's LJ."

We paused at the gate for Marcus to type in the entry code.

"We're off topic." I turned to Amelia. "What was going on at that bar?"

She looked away. "Nothing."

"So Marcus was throwing punches just for fun up there? I was told to run because you thought a late night jog was a good idea? Really?"

There was another huff of annoyance from the back seat. "It's not a big deal," Amelia said. "You know our Pete who works the Bubble Lounge?"

"The singer? Yeah." I nodded.

"He went off on that week-long fishing trip with the guys when we were down in New Zealand, right? Lost a ton of money playing poker."

Beside me Marcus made a noise of annoyance and muttered, "Learn to cut your losses. Tonnerre mes chiens!"[25]

"Pete settled up by betting them he could smuggle anything into Australia."

I muttered one of the better Cajun curses, which brought a sly smile to Marcus' face as we pulled up to the house.

"They gave Pete a small box—"

"—and you offered to help him," I finished for Amelia with another eye roll. If eye rolls kept you young, I was going to be a baby in no time. "Why? Please, please don't tell me it was the neighborly thing to do or you think Pete is cute. He's *old*."

"He's thirty-eight!" Amelia protested.

"And you're twenty-two. He's old enough to be your dad!"

"It's a sixteen-year age gap!"

"Plenty of people become parents at sixteen!"

"That's true," Marcus added.

I glared at him in the dim lights spilling from the house to the driveway. "You are not stupid, Amelia. Why'd you do this?"

---

[25] Literally: Thunder My Dogs! But it's basically the Cajun version of "for crying out loud!". Enough syllables to calm you down without being rude or mean.

She fidgeted with the box for a moment, then rolled her eyes. "He bet a hundred grand, in euros, that he could pull it off. He offered me a twenty percent cut. Easy money!"

"You gave it to me!" I shouted loud enough to make Marcus duck. "I'm not a native! If I got caught with something illegal, I'd lose my chance to stay here in Australia. No naturalization. No permanent address. Nothing. I'd probably have my bank accounts cut off too. That would leave me homeless and broke, back in the States."

"You have family," Amelia said, eyes wide and expression confused.

"I would rather die than be anywhere near my family," I said flatly. I opened the car door and stepped out, trying hard not to fume.

Marcus and Amelia were right behind me.

"It's not that big a risk," Amelia insisted. "It's not even anything illegal, I think."

"You think?" My shout echoed between the houses and I cringed. Poor little Robyn did not deserve this.

Marcus took the car key fob and tossed it to Amelia. "Go. Take the car. Go home to your parents' house. We'll talk about this tomorrow."

Amelia looked like she wanted to argue for a moment, but Marcus' look made her swallow anything she wanted to say. With a meek nod, she scurried back to the car.

A light breeze played around us, bringing the scent of the ocean and flowers.

"Are you okay?" Marcus asked as Amelia drove away.

"I should be asking you that," I said, belatedly realizing the darkness I saw on his face wasn't just shadows. "It looks like you got hit hard."

"Cher," he held his arms out wide as he smiled, "you know me. I wrestled in high school. I did jujitsu. I can take a punch. Right now, I'm worried about you. Do you want to come in?" He looked at the house.

I followed his gaze with a frown. "Why wouldn't I come in?"

"You sounded angry when Amelia said these were her kinfolk. You want to go? If you do, I'll get you a hotel for tonight. You don't need to stay here."

"No." I shook my head. "It's only for one more day. Robyn's expecting me for whatever is planned for tomorrow. I don't want to disappoint the kid."

"You sure?"

Frowning at him, I tried to guess why he was agitated. "Should I leave? Do you want me to?" A nasty suspicion made my gut churn. "Do you think Amelia did that 'cause of me?"

"No." Marcus shook his head, a frown of annoyance on his face that I'd seen on many a school day just before someone got a blackeye. "Amelia's..." He took a breath and scowled into the darkness after her. "Sometimes people get it into their head that money and shiny things are what matters most. They think having attention makes them important."

"We live in a capitalist society," I said flatly. "Having money and attention are how you survive. It's how you pay the bills."

He shook his head. "No. Not like that."

"It's how I pay my bills."

"Everything you do is legal. I'd bet my last dollar on that."

"Even knowing who my daddy is?"

Marcus snorted in amusement and turned back to me. "You're a lot of things, Lainey Jane, but you are nothing like that boot-faced warthog who thought he was your father."

I felt my cheeks heat. "That might be the nicest thing you've ever said to me."

He opened the door leading to the laundry room and the rest of the quiet house.

"Good night," I said before I could be tempted to let myself feel anything more.

"Good night, LJ," Marcus' voice floated after me into the darkness. "I'm sorry we didn't get our date. Maybe tomorrow?"

I hesitated for a moment, then nodded. "Tomorrow sounds good."

It was a risk, going out with Marcus, but it was one I was willing to take. There was more to him than I'd seen growing up, and I found myself wanting to discover all his hidden secrets.

TRYING HARD NOT TO IMAGINE A DATE WITH MARCUS DUPRE, I hurried upstairs and showered quickly, washing off the last of the bar and the last of the night. Turning off the light and closing the door to the bathroom, I retreated to my borrowed bed. It was comfy. Maybe I'd ask Madeleine in the morning where she'd gotten it. After all, with the money I was getting paid, I could finally buy my own bed.

Flopping between the soft pillows in the darkness I let myself daydream just a little.

I didn't want a cozy cottage with the white picket fence. But maybe an apartment with a park nearby. Some place where I could walk to the beach or over to the farmer's market. I wanted a living space with comfy couches and walls wide enough for unique art.

And... a treacherous thought swam through my mind as I pictured my future... room for someone else.

Someone in the kitchen helping me cook dinner. Someone who was excited when I came home. Someone who loved me.

My fantasy guy looked an awful lot like Marcus.

Groaning, I rolled over and buried my head under a pillow. This was such a bad idea. He was Marcus-Flipping-Dupre, prince of the swamps, king of the rabble. His father's kin had lived there since before Louisiana belonged to the US of A and his mother's people had lived "in and around the Gulf Coast" for longer than that. That was a direct quote.

The fact that I could still remember Marcus' presentation from fifth grade, and Miss Warbler correcting him by saying no one could "live in the Gulf Coast" really was a bad sign.

I did not want to be in love with Marcus Dupre.

Yes, right, he was handsome. Stunningly so.

Yes, true, he was a decent human being. Even as I dug through my worst memories, I couldn't think of a time he'd intentionally hurt me. He'd flirted with me like he flirted with everyone, but he'd never insulted me. Never thrown trash at me because my family was dirt poor and plain dirty. Never made me feel worthless.

That was the problem, really. Every time I had Marcus' full attention, it felt like he thought I was the most important person in the world, and I wasn't. Not by a long shot.

And I wasn't sure I could survive his disappointment when he realized I was nothing more than a dirty Pritchard.

It didn't matter that I didn't steal cars or run drugs like my brothers. I was still one of them. I ran half way around the world, changed hemispheres, and I still couldn't escape who I was born to. It was imprinted on me like my DNA and every day I worried I'd somehow slip up and become like them. Angry. Filthy. Vengeful. Cruel.

If I could jus—

My phone buzzed with a text, pulling me from my maudlin thoughts.

I rolled over again, pulled it off the nightstand, and checked to see who was texting me at midnight.

It was Amelia. "Hey, sheila, sorry about tonight," she wrote.

"No worries, mate," I typed back. After a moment I added, "You OK?"

Three little dots filled the screen as she started typing. "Yes," finally appeared.

"Really?"

More dots.

Then, "Ever feel like you've failed your family?"

"No," I replied honestly. "My family sucks."

An eyeroll GIF appeared.

"Mine's perfect," Amelia wrote. "Everyone is so good at everything. So smart. So rich. So pretty. I feel like a fake."

"You're smart and pretty too," I wrote back. "I don't know about your bank account, but I've never seen you worried about money."

This time she sent an upside down smiley emoji.

"That bad?" I asked.

"I may have done some gambling too," she admitted.

"How much?"

The dots lasted longer this time.

Minutes passed.

"Amelia?" I typed. "Can I help? If I gave you what I was getting paid this week?"

There was a pause, a flurry of dots, and then, "NO!"

"You sure?"

"You want a house," Amelia wrote back. "I don't want to get you involved. You deserve a better friend than me."

"You're a great friend," I replied. "Let me help. What can I do?"

The dreaded three dots reappeared.

Then, "If I can get this box to Peter's friends, I'm good. But Marcus has already told the family what happened tonight and my mum's fussing over me. She won't leave me alone."

I rolled my eyes. "Such a hardship to be loved!"

"It's smothering," Amelia wrote back. "I won't be able to get out. But I'll be at little Robyn's party tomorrow. I could give you the box..."

"...and I could deliver it?"

Falling back into the pillows, I debated the risks.

"We're deleting this text chain," I wrote back. "I don't want any proof I knew what was happening. I'm just doing a favor for a friend."

"Right," Amelia typed. "No one will know. You can go and I won't tell a soul you were involved. But, please, don't tell Marcus? Okay?"

I stared at the screen for a long moment as warning bells went off. "Why can't Marcus know?"

"Because he'll tell my da and then I'll be in heaps of trouble!"

"Right." I kept forgetting Amelia's idea of a worst case scenario was someone being cross with her.

"Please?" She added a weeping face emoji.

"Yes," I wrote back. "I promise this is just between us."

To prove it, I backed out of the app and deleted the whole chat thread so the last thing from Amelia was her asking me to come find her at the bar.

It was a bad idea. I knew it was a bad idea. But she was my friend. You had to help friends, right?

Plugging my phone in, I tried to shove aside the ominous feeling.

Keeping secrets should be easy for me, right? I had orchestrated the greatest escape from Pearl Rivers in generations! Helping a friend stay out of trouble shouldn't be that hard.

There was a thunk and a curse from the other side of the bathroom door.

I froze.

Another, quiet, Cajun curse.

Yelling would wake up the rest of the house, so I got up and quietly tapped on the door. "Marcus?"

A tension filled moment passed. "Cher?"

"Are you okay?"

Silence.

"Are you decent?" I asked.

"I've got pants on."

Before I could remember that *pants* was the British

term for underwear,[26] I opened the door to find Marcus Dupre sitting on the edge of the tub with his shirt off wearing nothing more than a scandalously short pair of black running shorts. The counter had gauze and some name brand goo meant to prevent infections.

"What happened?" I demanded as I flipped on the overhead light. "And why are you trying to work with the nightlight? The little mermaid in the corner holding a lantern fish is hardly enough to clean up after a bar fight."

"I didn't want to wake you up." He sounded apologetic.

"I wasn't asleep," I said. "Turn around."

He obediently turned, putting his feet in the tub and his back to me so I could see a large gash in his right shoulder.

"Was this from tonight?"

"Yeah." He glanced back at me. "I thought someone had hit me until I showered and saw blood. It stings, but it's not deep."

"Did someone really knife you?"

"Might have been an edge of a chair leg or something." He shrugged and then hissed at the pain. "I've had worse. It's no worry."

"I know you've had worse. I had to pick up the bar after a couple of your *worse* nights."

"Wasn't me that started them fights, cher."

Ignoring his protests, I grabbed the cleaning supplies. "This will sting."

"Want to kiss it better?"

"The urge to smack the back of your head is strong."

He chuckled. "Don't want to kiss it better?"

"I've never known kissing to fix much of anything," I grumbled as I washed out the cut.

"Ooo, cher, you do sound bitter. You need help feeding some couyon[27] to the sharks? Some fool boy done gone

---

[26] Something I learned from a British shipmate named Dane the hard way.

[27] It's Cajun slang for fool or bastard. Pronounced *coo-yaaawawn.*

and broken your heart?"

"That assumes I had a heart to begin with," I said as I leaned over to look him in the eye, "and we both know I don't have that."

Marcus' smile was wickedly confident. Slow to start, but as steady and strong as he was. He held eye contact as he rolled his shoulders back. "Sure thing, cher, you lie all you like. I saw how you were treating Robyn and her little mermaids. How you went rushing into trouble for Amelia."

I looked away before he could guess how much trouble I was rushing into.

"You can play tough with the best of 'em, but you've got a soft heart in there somewhere."

Snorting in dismissal, I grabbed the bandages from the counter. "Wishful thinking, Mister Dupre."

"Ah, cher! You wound me!" He clutched his hands to his chest playfully. "All these years of me pining like a crane that done lost its mate."[28]

"I'm sure you can find someone to repair it for you." I plastered on the last of the bandage and patted his shoulder. "Plenty of people around here would love to comfort a Cajun."

He caught my hand and turned, looking up at me with soulful eyes. "Would I ever be enough for you, Lainey?" He sounded serious.

All of a sudden it seemed like the room was missing oxygen.

Marcus Dupre and Serious weren't words I ever

---

[28] Whooping cranes were a common sight in the bayou and rather famously mated for life. Our sixth-grade biology class had been lucky enough to see a pair doing a mating dance and we'd gotten updates on them from our science teacher until she retired when I was in tenth grade.

thought would be combined, unless it was along the lines of *Serious Injury*.

"All these years, and you push me away like I'm no more than swamp trash." His laugh was bitter and heartbroken. "Don't matter what kind words I use or how I say them. You always blow past me like a tempest on a Tuesday."

I shook my head, not sure where he was going with this.

"Is it my family? My roots?"

"No." I shook my head again. "Your family is fine. They seem nice."

"Is it me? My looks? The fact I like everyone? Too many past lovers?"

"No." Tugging my hand away seemed mean, so I held still. "It's just... you flirt with everyone. I know it's how you are. I'm not going to pretend it means anything. I don't expect anything from you."

He tilted his head, the blue sparks in his eyes looking like lightning in the dark of a storm. "What if I meant it?"

My heart raced at the possibility.

"What if I flirted with you because I want you in my life, Lainey Jane? What if I wanted to be more to you than just *that boy you went to school with*? Would you want that too?"

"I don't know." I pulled my hand away. "You're handsome. You're charming. You're Marcus Dupre, the boy every girl in the parish wanted. But I'm just LJ."

"I don't want you to be anyone but LJ."

"Yeah, but I'm not sure the LJ you want is who I really am. I'm not that quiet little girl who did whatever she was told and never talked back."

His smile almost broke me. "Cher, you were never quiet. Poor Brandy Simineaux[29] got her teeth knocked out

---

[29] Simineaux is pronounced Sim-In-Oh.

by you because she told you that you were no better than that good-for-nothing daddy you had."

"I got suspended for a week for that," I said bitterly. "And got a thrashing from my dad because it brought child services 'round."

"Learning to pick your fights doesn't mean you don't have fight in ya. It means you're playing smart."

"But, that's the thing. I don't want to play. I don't want a future of fights and fists. I want a house, and friends, and a life where I am loved for being myself. I want someone who knows my favorite color, my favorite song, my favorite food. I want to come home to someone who is happy when I'm happy, and who makes plans with me instead of just ordering me around. I don't want to be a waitress or the hired help. I want a home where I'm an equal."

Marcus stood, towering over me.

The silence stretched between us as I realized I'd just told the handsomest man ever born in St. Tammany Parish that he wasn't enough for me.

"Yellow," Marcus said, "and sunrise purple, with a bit of pink in it. *Shooting Stars* by J-Slay the rapper. Chewy caramels with dark chocolate." The corner of his mouth lifted in a smile. "Good night, LJ. Have good dreams." He leaned forward and brushed a kiss on my cheek, then turned and left the bathroom, closing the door.

Even though I owned a lot of yellow and loved it, sunrise purple was my secret favorite color. J-Slay, the Japanese rapper, was my favorite artist and *Shooting Stars* was the new song he'd released last year; it was my favorite. Dark chocolate-covered chewy caramels were always my favorite treat.

I wiped away a tear.

No one in my life had ever known all three.

Marcus Dupre did.

I didn't know what to do with that.

My last day of being Robyn's mermaid bestie was a blur of visitors, an afternoon sausage sizzle, and a frenzied hunt for new accommodations. Amelia had promised I could stay in the guest house for the duration of our holiday, but since the tree had taken out the roof and I wasn't keen to stay in the guest room in the main house, I needed to find somewhere else to go.

I'd asked Amelia about it when she stopped by with her parents before lunch, but she'd shrugged it off, slid the package to me, and vanished.

Since it was the holiday season in Sydney I was also competing with everyone else in the world, apparently. I'd go to book a room and between entering my credit card number and clicking *Book*, the hotel would sell out. By the time the family was getting ready to go out for dinner, I was beginning to think I'd be sleeping out on the beaches.

There was a knock at the bedroom door.

"Yes?" I looked up. "Come on in."

Madeleine pushed the door open, blonde hair pulled back in a ponytail. "Hiya. I was coming to give you the last of your pay. Amelia was planning to stay in the guest house so she didn't need to stay with her parents; were you planning to stay too, or do you have family in town?"

"I was going to stay, but I'm working on booking a hotel now," I said, holding up my phone just as it flashed red and told me there were no more vacancies at a run-down hotel nearly an hour away. "If I can't find anything I'll reach out to the cruise line and see if one of the smaller cruises has room for me. I can go back to work early." Unfun, but practical.

"Oh! No!" Madeleine shook her head. "We promised you a place to stay. The guest house is out, but we've got a company apartment downtown that we use for remote workers who are coming in for conferences and whatnot. It's open until mid-January. Why not stay there?"

"How much?" I asked.

She shook her head with a confused frown. "No cost to you! You can move into tomorrow arvo. It means staying another night here, but I think Robyn's really taken a shine to you. Would that be okay?"

"If it works for you, yeah, I'm... that'd be great!" The pesky little box weighed on my conscience. "I was going to go out tonight to meet some friends. I can find a hotel tonight, if you want. I'm nearly packed."

Madeleine shook her head. "No, no, no. No worries! I'll give you my number and I can buzz you in when you get back. Do you need to borrow a car?"

"Nah. I'll take a taxi." Borrowing a car was overkill. Especially since she'd already paid me so well. This was starting to sound like a bargain with the fey. I didn't read much, but the fairies had been a popular topic in YA books and TV shows back when I was in high school and I knew accepting gifts was dangerous.

That probably didn't hold true for accepting gifts from Australians, but you could never be too careful.

"Sounds good." Madeleine's smile widened. "Thank you for doing all this for Robyn this week. It's really helped her."

"I'm glad." I also desperately wanted to ask why the family was so worried about Robyn if it wasn't a terminal illness, but no one was dropping hints like they wanted to share, so I was keeping my nosiness to myself. If they wanted to tell me, they would.

Hesitating like she wanted to say something more, Madeleine hovered for an awkward moment in the doorway, then re-upped the mega-wattage of her smile, shrugged, and turned to go down the hall.

I kicked the door closed as my phone rang with Amelia's ringtone.

"I swear," I said, "if I need to come rescue you agai—"

"No!" She sounded bothered and upset, but not angry. "No, I was calling to talk to you about tonight. I think, maybe, it would be better to just lose the bet, you know? I can make the money some other time."

"It's no biggie," I said, flopping back on my borrowed bed. "The mermaid party is over. The whole family is going out to dinner with some grandparents somewhere."

Somewhere expensive, by the way they were getting dressed up.

There was a grumble from Amelia's end of the line.

"Are you supposed to be going to the dinner?"

"Yeah," she admitted with a heavy sigh. "The whole family'll be there. Including a cousin who's now married to one of my exes."

I winced on her behalf. "Eww. Sorry."

It was easy to picture her eye roll. "Nah. It'll be fine," she said in the tone of voice she used when picking up her week's worth of dirty socks because she wanted to avoid the conversation.

Seriously, there were times when Amelia seemed more like a long-lost sister than simply my work bestie. She mimicked my brother's behaviors often enough that I found myself falling into the same habits I'd used to survive them.

That was another thing to bring up with my therapist next week. I wasn't supposed to be Amelia's caretaker. I was her friend, not her parent or guardian.

Cutting off a growl, I forced a happier tone. "It'll be fine. After all, you're not paying are you?"

Amelia laughed. "No! Thank guppies! I know that side of the family has more money than we do, but, ugh!" Her eye roll was almost audible. "This is beyond ridiculous."

"Order extra dessert for me," I said as I heard someone calling Amelia's name from her end of the line. "Have a fin-tastic time! Make some mermaid-a-rific memories!" Laughing at our usual sign off to the kids on the cruise, I hung up.

All that was left to do was get dressed for the night, order a car, and go get rid of this infernal box before I got cursed with whatever bad luck was stalking Amelia.

My outfit for the evening was a yellow halter dress with tiger lilies and a flared skirt. The little black shorts underneath kept it safe enough for wearing out and it went with my cute white-and-yellow tennis shoes.

If things didn't go well I'd try a charm offensive.

If that didn't work, I'd run.

When the taxi said it was ten minutes out, I hurried down the stairs, intent on getting to the front gate before my ride. I came to a screeching halt in the front entry way, centimeters away from crashing into a man in a stunning dark blue suit with a gray-and-blue tie that was, as it turned out, interlayered sharks in a repeating pattern. Something I would have never noticed if I was not dan-gerously close to colliding with the person who'd stepped in front of me.

I looked up into chocolate-brown eyes with the flashes of blue that always captured my attention. "Marcus."

He looked me up and down, expression guarded.

Oops.

There was no way to miss that he looked like a million bucks and I didn't even look like this dress was worth a hundred. Mostly because I'd grabbed it from the trash pile after it lived in the cruise's lost-and-found pile for six months.

"You look good," he said, voice truly neutral. "Are you coming to dinner with us?"

"Nope." I pushed my bag to the side just in case he remembered the size of the box he didn't want Amelia having and realized that the little canvas tote[30] I was using as a purse would fit the box perfectly. "I'm meeting some friends for dinner. Then I move out in the morning."

He nodded slowly. "Good. Sounds fun."

"Yup." Nodding in return, I stepped around him—but a question that had been absolutely nagging me since the night before had to get answered. "Last night—"

"Yes?"

I turned, frowning. "How'd you know what my favorite song was? It's not the one I listed in the high school yearbook. I don't have social media as myself, only as one of the Merry Mermaids. So what did you do? Read my mind? Guess? List your favorite?"

That was a tantalizing idea.

If we liked the same music, well, maybe there was a connection there? Maybe?

The sexy Cajun smile I'd always known Marcus Dupre to have slowly spread across his face. "You kept singing along with it. Every time it came on the radio at the beach. You danced to it in the car even when you were trying to ignore me."

"Maybe I just think it's a catchy song."

He lifted a shoulder in a shrug. "It fits you."

So it wasn't his favorite. That... kind of hurt, actually. I wanted us to have something in common and we didn't.

Nodding, I turned away, heading to the door.

"LJ?"

I froze, hand on the door handle.

---

[30] With a map of Thailand on it.

"Do you still want to have dinner together?" He sounded more guarded and sad than I'd ever heard him.

"Do you?"

"I would."

I nodded. "Then we'll do dinner sometime before you leave. You can get my number from Amelia when you see her tonight."

Rushing out the door before he could say anything else was cowardly, but I needed to escape. Marcus gave me so many conflicting feelings that staying was out of the question. Besides, the cab was waiting. The sooner I got rid of this cursed box, the sooner I could move on.

I'd have dinner with Marcus and finally close the door on my old life.

And, if something sparked while we were out? Well, then I'd start a new life. One with a happier ending.

A WARM, OCEAN-SCENTED BREEZE FLITTED PAST THE HARBOR BAR where Amelia was planning to meet her contact. The party here was already in full swing when I arrived, even though it wasn't even full dark yet. Pop music with a Christmas-y winter theme was blasting and the special drink of the night was something called Snowman's Delight, which looked like coconut milk mixed with something and carrot shreds on top.

I'm not sure how it was meant to be delightful but I did belly up to the bar long enough to order some prawns and french fries. There were times when I missed Cajun cooking. Tonight was one of those times.

Not bothering to finish the overcooked prawns and the cold fries, I walked around the edges of the dance floor that was on a patio overlooking the docks. Nice little mini-yachts lined the rows of the wooden wharf.

Someone yelled "Next round on me!" to the cheers of the crowd as a live band came out to start playing.

Since there were free drinks, I circled back. There were milkshakes on the menu and I figured that could tide me over until I got back to the house and raided my stash of snacks.

Tomorrow I'd have to figure out my living situation for the next eleven days and hit the grocery store. Then I'd be back on the ship for my final cruise. My future was looking bright.

All I had to do was get through one more night of running errands for friends and bunking near Marcus.

As I approached the bar, the barkeep looked up and smiled at me. "Hey."

"Hi." I smiled back.

The barkeep held out a phone. "Looking for your phone?"

"What?" I thought I'd misheard him over the noise.

"The guy who just left said the sheila in the yellow dress dropped this." The barkeep held out a phone in a battered gray case that looked old as a tortoise.

I started shaking my head to explain.

"No worries." The barkeep tossed me the phone and winked. "You can leave me the number if you want me to call later. Coming right up!" he hollered to someone waving further down the bar.

Staring at the phone, I wondered if I should just drop it off or if the barkeep would keep trying to give it to me.

The phone rang with a standard ringtone.

Probably the owner calling from a friend's phone as they tried to find this. I answered. "Hello?"

There was a hushed pause. "You Amelia's friend?"

Ah. So, not an accidental drop. I crossed my arms and pressed up against the bar, scanning the crowd as I tried to figure out who was calling.

"Are you?" the man pressed.

"I am."

"Good. Pier four, slip four-fourteen. At the end on the left. Meet our man down there in the next ten minutes or the deal's off." He hung up before I could argue.

"Sorry about the interruption," the barkeep said behind me.

I turned to him, holding out the phone. "This isn't mine."

Confusion contorted his face. "But you answ—"

"I thought the owner was calling. It wasn't, it was a stalker." Close enough to the truth, even if they were more Amelia's stalker at this point. "Can you call the police or something? I was supposed to meet someone for a date, but he's not here and I don't want to be here either."

"Want me to call you a cab?" the barkeep asked.

"That'd be great. Thank you."

"It'll take about twenty minutes," he warned.

"No worries. I'm just going to step into the loo for a minute." I glanced to the narrow hall where a line of ladies were already waiting.

"There's another downstairs by the picnic benches. Our downstairs window is closed until after ten, so there shouldn't be too many people there."

Smiling, I nodded. "Thanks. The cab's for LJ."

"Twenty minutes," he promised. "It'll be at the front drop-off point."

"Thank you."

At least four minutes had gone by and I wasn't sure how punctual Amelia's pal was going to be, so I hustled down the stairs outside. The bar was near pier ten.

It was Christmas Eve and crowded out, but the crowds thinned by pier six and by pier four I was in the shadows of an office building and everyone was elsewhere. I was feeling very grateful for my sneakers at this point because I didn't think charm would work.

The sun was sinking over the western hills[31] but it wasn't full dark yet.

Long shadows stretched under a blood-stained sky along the pier as the boats rocked gently in their slips. These weren't fancy mini-yachts or speed boats; they looked more like work ships. A couple of them had SCUBA equipment in lockers on their decks. Others had signs for harbor tours and fishing charters. All of them felt like the kind of small, family businesses you'd expect to see at small docks around the world.

---

[31] Yes, as shocking as this may sound to Americans, Sydney is an east coast city and the sun doesn't set over the water.

At the far end of the pier, a heavyset man waited in the shadows. He was around six-foot tall and, I was guessing, outweighed me by at least a hundred pounds. I could run if I needed to, and in a pinch I could dive into the water and I hope I was the better swimmer, but I didn't want to get into a fist fight with this guy.

Here, away from the evening crowds, I expected to hear some shore birds. Maybe see a seagull or two. But they'd apparently ditched me to go chase french fries near the restaurants, so even if I screamed I wouldn't set them into a flurry and draw attention.

Maybe I should have brought back up.

I'd never really had anyone to rely on, but right in this moment, I wished I did. It would be very reassuring to have Marcus beside me. Or Amelia. Or, heck, right now I'd take Gamblin' Pete or Jenni from the bar in Pearl River.

Aware that time was ticking, I squared my shoulders and headed toward the man standing in the shadows, doing my very best to look unafraid and unbothered.

"Lainey Jane." The accent was a poor man's American Southern. A bit of Texas. A bit of Oklahoma. A bit of Bayou. A lot of hate.

Beau stood in front of me.

"That's not my name." I held out the box Amelia had given me. "This yours? Or is Amelia's friend someone else?"

"Elaine Janine Pritchard," Beau said, cruelty painting every word with vibrant hatred. "That's no way to greet family."

"Still not my name," I insisted. "And you're not my family." And Amelia wasn't my friend. That backstabbing little sea snake!

Beau's lips twitched up in a vicious smile as he snatched the box. "I thought that pretty little girl was full of it," he said as he opened the box and pulled out a fan.

We'd done all this for a *fan*? I was going to give my roommate such an earful.

Then find another roommate.

"But she was showing my pictures on her phone and what did I see? Why—" Beau tossed the fan on the pier and pulled out his brand new, top-of-the-line phone and turned it to me to show a picture of me and Amelia in Singapore. "That there's my baby sister! All gussied up and forgetting her roots."

"Enjoy your delusions," I said. "I'm not your sister and I have a cab waiting."

"But you are." Beau stepped closer. "We got the same dee-en-ay."

The way he said it made my blood run cold. "So? How does that matter?"

"Well, you see," he tucked his phone away and rested his thumbs in the front pockets of his jeans the way our grandpa did before he started lecturing us as kids, "you are in a bit of a pickle. Went missing without warning."

"I was a legal adult. I was allowed to move out at any time."

"Cost the parish a bit of money, looking for you."

"I doubt that very much."

"Cost the family even more. We had to move because of you."

"Any of you could have paid the rent if you wanted to."

"Now you're in a foreign country."

"I have a work visa."

"With a criminal background."

The words sunk into the growing darkness around us.

I shook my head. "No. I don't have a criminal back-ground."

"Oh, but you do," Beau insisted. "You racked up all sorts of credit cards. Then there's the fraud." He let out a low whistle. "Lost money left and right. Whoo-whee! It was bad. You were a terrible, terrible person Lainey Jane."

"That's. Not. My. Name," I ground out, wishing I had a way to make him vanish forever. "I moved out. I got a job. I changed my name. I created a life for myself and you cannot drag me back."

"But I can. If I want, I can absolutely turn you over to the authorities. There might even be a reward for it. Louisiana does not take kindly to scam artists." Beau's smile turned almost happy. "But I won't. 'Cause I'm your big brother and I love you so. You want to live here in the land of the crocodiles and giant spiders? You go right ahead."

"Good. Because I intend to."

"All you have to do is bring me one teensy-weensy little thing from that house you're staying at. There's a couple of things on their business computer we need."

I stared at him in confusion.

Beau's smile turned predatory. "See, we're doing salvage. So are the Dupre's, in Louisiana and here. But there was a tiny bit of confusion and they picked up some cargo that wasn't meant for them back in Joo-lie," he dragged the word July out as if it had special meaning.

"So?"

"So, they made the terrible mistake of turning that cargo over to the police and..." Beau hissed, then clicked his tongue as he shook his head. "Let's say some of our clients were none too happy with that choice. The Dupres need to learn a lesson. Be brought down a peg or two. Shouldn't be problem for you, should it? You never did get along with them."

I shook my head. "I'm not involved with this."

"You are," Beau insisted. "You're going to do the family one last favor. You go into the computer, put this in there," he held up a USB3 drive, "and you run the program. Then get me any maps or charts you find. Do that, and we'll call it good."

"No," I repeated. "I am not stealing from someone."

"You already did," Beau said. "One little call to the police, and you're going back to a Louisiana prison for life. They don't take kindly to people stealing from little old ladies down there. And, hoo boy! Did you steal a lot!"

A cold certainty settled over me. "You used my old name and set up accounts."

"Set up bank accounts, credit cards, all sorts of things," Beau said with a nod. "All in your name. So you're going to take the fall. Australia won't let you stay. America's prison system wants you. By New Year's you can have a bright orange jumpsuit or—"

He held up the thumb drive.

"Do what you're told, Elaine. The family is gone for most the night. You can get in, get the information, and get out tomorrow with no one being the wiser. You go your way. We'll go ours. Promise."

"I don't trust your promises."

"Trust this: you have twelve hours. If this isn't back in my hands by then, I'm reporting you to the police. You can run as far as you want, but they'll freeze your bank account. You'll lose your visa and your job." He waggled the USB3 drive so it caught the light. "One little thing that won't hurt you at all, or the next ten years in prison?"

I held out my hand. "I hate you."[32]

"Merry Christmas to you too, kiddo. One of us will meet you here tomorrow. Before lunch. We've got things to do."

Fighting back tears, I turned and headed to my doom.

-----

[32] And also hated the fact that this was a problem I could solve with a plastic drum, a bit of cement, and shoving the whole kit-n-kaboodle over the side of the cruise ship when we hit international waters. Murder wasn't the right answer, but it was a tempting one.

All the way back to the house, I fought tears. What was I supposed to do?

What *could* I do?

If I got the data, it would be a crime my family could hold over me, and the Dupres weren't stupid. Once Marcus' family realized someone had broken in, they'd figure out who. It wasn't like there were a lot of options. It was me or Marcus, and Marcus was out with the family tonight, giving him an alibi no one would question.

If I didn't get the data, I had no doubts my brother would report me to some police somewhere. Why bother creating a criminal record for me if they didn't intend to use it?

Yes, when I went before the judge I could argue the accounts were fake. With a decent lawyer I might even be free. But that assumed the judge, the lawyer, the court, the prison, and everyone in between hadn't been bought off by my father to make sure I was punished. One corrupt judge who didn't bother wanting to hear my story. One bad lawyer paid to look the other way. One angry cellmate looking for a little cash... and I was dead.

The only reasonable thing to do was run.

Madeleine had paid me well. I could leave tonight, fly somewhere, anywhere. Send an email quitting the cruise line and look for work somewhere else. I probably wouldn't graduate like I wanted, but that was a secondary concern. I needed to get out of here. Go somewhere land-locked maybe.

Somewhere where mermaids and boats and marine salvage were all equally fantastical ideas.

By the time I'd made it back to the quiet house on Mermaid Lane, it was full dark. The silent tears I'd cried in the back of the cab had stopped streaming, and I had a *plan*.

Or at least the "pla" of a "plan".

A few years back, someone had asked me if I wanted to nanny. I was good with kids. I could go be a nanny somewhere for a few years. Finish up my accounting degree online. Apply for citizenship somewhere my family wasn't going to find me.

I took the stairs two at a time in the darkness, tossed my yellow suitcase on the bed without turning on the lamps, and started packing in the moonlight like the thief I was.

There was a knock at the bedroom door.

"It's open." If Madeleine asked when she came in, I'd tell her I was getting ready for tomorrow. "I didn't hear the car pull up."

"I got dropped off." Marcus' voice behind me made me freeze.

For a long moment I waited for some sign from the universe about what to do.

Nothing happened, so I finished tucking away my toiletries before I turned, expression neutral. "How'd the dinner go?"

"Fine." Marcus' tone suggested this was a lie. He switched on the hall light so the golden glow fell across the floor.

"I thought you were staying out until midnight," I said, trying to keep my stage smile in place. "I heard something about family traditions."

He lifted a shoulder in a shrug and looked past me out the window. "Normally, true. Tonight," his eyes met mine, "Amelia had a bit of a breakdown. Ran off. Said summin' that didn't quite make sense. Her ma and pa went home looking for her. Grandpa sent me here. To see if she'd come talk to you. Seemed she was worried about you."

No *cher* on the end of that sentence, I noticed.

I couldn't help but feel a little deflated. When it came down to the wire, Marcus had his family and they weren't mine. And they weren't welcoming.

"You wanna chime in here?" Marcus asked, hands in his back pockets as if they were trying to hold himself back from grabbing me.

"Nope." I shook my head and went to the closet to grab the last of my shirts. "I'm just packing for the move tomorrow. Madeleine has some other place for me."

Marcus sighed and ran a hand through his hair. "Huh. Right. So, no other concerns?"

"I don't see how anything I do would be your concern at all. I'm not family." That came out a little more bitterly than I meant it to.

"You could be," Marcus said. "Say the word, cher, and I'll be down on one knee with the diamond of your choosing."

Rolling my eyes, I looked at him with a laugh. "You're going to propose to me without even going on a date? Are you desperate? Are you under some curse where you need to marry before age thirty or you die? Is this one of those fantasy movies where you can smell your mate across the room?"

Marcus laughed with me, but his eyes were darkly serious. "No, cher. It's nothing like that. Just good, ol' fashioned want-you-to-be-mine. Every time I think I've almost got a chance, got a dinner lined up, promised I can take you out for a drink... you vanish." He paused, watching me fold another t-shirt and tuck it away.

"It's a little scary. Last time I thought you died. Here tonight?" He nodded to my suitcase. "Looks to me like you might vanish all over again."

"This is just..." I looked at the suitcase. "Um..."

Duck me in a pond, he was right.

Marcus Dupre was a decent human being and I was getting ready to vanish on him. That probably wasn't healthy. For either of us.

"Can you wait?" he asked. "At least until Amelia has a chance to apologize?"

I raised my eyebrows in surprise. "You want me to wait for Amelia? Why?" I wanted to ask what he knew, but that would require admitting I knew something.

"What do you know about Amelia?" Marcus asked the one question I desperately wanted to avoid as he leaned back against the door frame, not quite blocking my exit, still giving me plenty of space to move around the room.

"She's very outgoing." I finished folding my t-shirt as I thought. "Her favorite nail polish is called Whimsy Pink. She hates orange juice unless it's fresh squeezed. She can do a ton of accents."

"What do you know about her past?" Marcus sounded way too serious for a casual question.

I shook my head. "Not much. She told me her family weren't super happy with her when she joined the mermaid show."

"No. They were happy for the show," Marcus said. "They were upset because she was there because she was an addict."

"What?" I tried to picture Amelia addicted to anything beyond counting tips and couldn't. "No. I'm furious with Amelia for setting me up tonight, but she's not an addict. She doesn't do drugs. She may have gambled once or twice, but she's really organized. Very focused. Best-foot-forward type of person."

Marcus nodded. "She is. Now. Because of you."

I shook my head again. "I had nothing to do with that."

"You did." He shifted his weight, taking the smallest of steps forward as he maintained eye contact. "The cruise line you work for, do you know who founded it?"

"No." Another tiny shake. "I knew they paid well and I didn't ask any other questions. I didn't want to get into the illegal side of things."

"They're legal. They're a cruise line and rehab clinic. All the workers, or almost all the workers, have prior addictions and are trying to get clean. My family researched it extensively for Amelia. The first few months she was there, she hated it. Then, suddenly, she was all smiles. There was this new girl at work. Someone who understood her. Someone who talked to her all the time. Someone who could fake a smile for the worst customers and always had good news to share."

"Who the duck was that?" I demanded as I mentally listed everyone on the ship. My co-workers weren't all cranky curmudgeons but I couldn't think of one who was all smiles all the time.

"You."

"Me?" I laughed. "I'm not an always-cheerful kind of person. You know that."

He nodded. "I do. But you're also unfailingly kind to people."

"I'm really not."

A soft smile spread across his lips in a way that made me wish this conversation wasn't about anyone but us. "You're kind, LJ. You take care of people. You make them feel seen. Poor little Robyn has been stressed for months, feeling sick with worry. Three days with you and she has hope again. Amelia hated her job, was ready to run off and go back to drugs. She met you and she's made it to her three year sober mark without any troubles."

"Oh, she had troubles."

"Smuggling." The way he said it didn't make it sound like a guess.

"It was a fan," I said. "A little hand fan."

"An expensive museum piece well over the import limits. It should have been declared at the border."

"But it's also an easy thing to overlook," I argued. "Customs wouldn't notice it even if it came through the airport."

Marcus twitched an eyebrow up in amusement. "The fact that the person she was giving it to was a Pritchard made no never mind?"

My heart sank. "You knew?"

"Amelia said something about your brother wanting contact. Said something about a bad feeling about it." He shrugged. "I know your brothers, cher. They aren't good men."

"So..." I tossed the shirts I was holding into my suitcase.

"So," Marcus repeated. "Are you going to let me help?"

I stared at him in the moonlit shadows of the room. It would have been romantic under other circumstances, if we weren't discussing blackmail and betrayal. If I wasn't at least thirty percent certain Marcus would abandon me when this was over.

He took another step toward me. "I know you're yer own woman"—he was quoting me—"and you can handle your own fights. But, maybe, for this, could you use some back up?"

Exactly what I'd wanted earlier. I sighed. "My brother wants me to get shipping data off the computer in the office downstairs," I admitted. "Some-thing about revenge for a shipping container Madeleine's company pulled up in July that had something they were smuggling. I'd bet my bottom dollar my brothers are run-ning bootlegs where they dump cargo off the ship some-where in international waters, not too deep, and the salvage company picks it up and brings it in. Or loads it onto another ship headed where they need it to go. It's easy enough money."

"Do you need to help them?"

"Yes." I grimaced as I grabbed my socks from the dresser. "Apparently, when I left, they ran a bunch of scams in my name. Racked up fraud charges. Enough to have me shipped back to the States if they reported me. Chances are good they already bought a judge to give me the verdict they want in court. My father was always good about paying the authorities the bribes they wanted to look the other way."

"So," Marcus looked at the suitcase, "you're packing to leave?"

"I'm packing. If I leave now I might be able to catch a flight out of here before I'm reported and deported. I can go somewhere else. Japan, maybe. Or the Philippines, that'd be cheaper. I'll earn some money and start over. Go find a place with less coastline. Hope I never see them again."

Marcus raised an eyebrow in a skeptical look. "How long you gonna keep running, Lainey Jane?" He was dangerously close now.

If he reached out, he'd be able to touch me.

If he reached out...

I looked away. "I'll keep running as long as I need to."

He reached, taking the socks from my hand. "You don't need to run."

Tears of panic blurred my vision. "I do. I really do. There's no other way out of this."

"You could ask for help." His eyes met mine. His voice was heartbreakingly patient.

"From who?"

"Me." He was a breath away. Close enough to kiss. "Why won't you ask me for help?"

The gentleness in his voice broke me.

"Because everyone who was ever supposed to help me abandoned me. Because I'm unlovable. Because no one ever, ever wanted to be there for me." I closed my eyes, remembering what he'd said at that last day at the bar. "At least, that's how I saw it. It was always Lainey Jane against the world. If you were there for backup, I missed it. Every time. I'm sorry."

"I'm sorry I didn't do a good enough job." His hand brushed along my shoulder in a gentle, reassuring pat. "We were young. I didn't know how to be who you needed then. I'm not sure I'm perfect now, but can you let me try? Let me try to be who you need?"

"And... what if we fail? My family is bent on destroying me. They're mad they lost their built-in maid and servant. I was their bank, their cook, and their cleaner, and then I left."

Marcus slipped his hand around my waist, pulling me close. "We're not going to fail. We're going to get you safely away from them, put them in jail, and make sure you have the life you want. Then? We're going to dinner."

"Promise?" I put my arms around his neck in a hug because it felt natural.

"Promise."

For the first time since I was a child, I leaned into someone. I rested my head on Marcus' shoulder and let him hold me as I cried. Just this once, I would believe someone would help me.

It is a truth universally acknowledged that liars and cheats expect to be lied to and cheated on.

It is also a truth universally acknowledged that everyone can change. Sometimes it isn't as easy as taking a mermaid tail off, but it is possible for everyone. They just have to *want* to change.

My father didn't want to change.

He was one the world's biggest liars and proud of it. Lying was so natural to him that he thought everyone else was a liar too, and so he was suspicious of me stalling the next morning when I didn't have anything for him before breakfast.

I bought him off with the picture of a shipping invoice that showed where a shipment of luxury goods was lost at sea and the plan to pick them up last week with a mark reading Storm Delay.

The weather was easy to check, and the rough seas combined with the holidays meant no one was likely to have rushed out this week to get things. Although Marcus shrugged that off, saying the goods had been retrieved.

Either the ships from Madeleine's Brightwater Salvage got in and out before the storm, or their team could perform some kind of magic. I didn't know if I believed either were possible, but with Marcus' go-ahead, I sent the info and got the response.

Nine that night.

Another marina, north of the city this time.

All the documents, or my father was going to start leaking information to the Aussie government and my employer.

It wasn't much, but it was enough time to thank Madeleine for her hospitality, get paid the last of what I was owed, tell Robyn goodbye, and move my gear to the guest room downtown.

Now, a cool breeze blew in from the south, a quiet reminder that Australia was a lot closer to an arctic tundra than I'd imagined as a kid. The dock here was older, with less boats in the slips and more decay in the wooden boards.

Somewhere in the distance, a car honked its horn and I caught the smell of my youngest older brother's dollar-store cologne. He'd worn it since high school, and it smelled like a car air freshener stirred into the cheapest booze in the world.

"I'm here," I said to the darkness, stopping midway down the dock.

Bobby stepped into the low lights coming off another ship. "Long time no see, baby sister." His sneer was as cruel and greedy as always. "I ought to give you a black eye for all the trouble you've caused."

"You ought to give me a handwritten thank you note for buying you groceries for five years," I said as I held out the packet. "Here's what you wanted. Papers. USB3 drive with all the data. Everything I could find in their home office."

"Any trouble?" he asked as he took the packet.

I shook my head. "There was a lock, but I told the lady I thought I'd heard weird beeping in the room. She was drunk from her dinner party so she went in, turned off the security, and I kept the door open so it didn't reset."

"Looks like we trained you well."

"Or I've seen a spy movie," I retorted as I tossed the packet to him. "Have a good life. I hope to never see you again."

Before I could even turn he grabbed my arm, gripping it tight enough to bruise. "Funny thing," Bobby said. "It's Christmas back home in the States."

"That's funny how?"

"We're all here today, see? Dad. Your brothers. You."

I tried to shake his grip. "Thanks. I pass."

His hand tightened. "You don't get to make that decision, Janey. Get onboard."

Several watery curses crossed my lips. "Let go."

"Or what?" My brother shoved me toward the boat. "You'll call the police? Do it. I'd love to see you in jail. It would make you grow up."

"I'm perfectly grown up as I am."

"You're a lazy good-for-nothin' who left your family!"

"I was a legal adult who moved into her own house so I could keep my own paycheck!" I hollered back. "What I earn, I'm allowed to keep. You don't own me."

Bobby shoved me toward the boat. "All those years of looking after you. Of making sure you got to school. Paying for your lunches."

"That's what parents do," I shot back. "If Mom and Dad didn't want me, they should have given me to someone else. They didn't. That's on them."

"You used my money!"

"Your money?" I stared at him for a moment wondering if he could hear himself. "Your money? You never earned a penny in your life! If you did, you turned right around and gave it to the nearest dealer of whatever you were using that week."

The look in his eyes turned vicious. "I'm owed! I worked for this family! I did what I was told! I'm owed some happiness!"

"If you want happiness, you need rehab."

Bobby pulled me close enough that I could smell the weed on his breath. "You always were a spoiled brat.

Selfish. An uppity little—" He shoved me toward the gang plank. "Get on board. Why Dad wants you alive is a mystery. But he's going to get what he wants. For now." Bobby's scowl promised swift retaliation as soon as my father's protection was removed.

None of this was new.

It was exactly the welcome I'd gotten from my brother hundreds of times. But, after three years away from him, it was worse.

I could still remember when I got my babysitting job at twelve. I was so proud I'd earned thirty dollars. I walked into the hellishly smelly little doublewide we owned, excited and expecting to be praised, when Bobby ambushed me.

He'd jumped off the couch and pawed at my purse like some deranged dog, demanding to know how much I'd earned. When he saw it was only thirty dollars, he'd backhanded me as he'd yelled that it wasn't enough, he needed at least fifty for a hit of the good stuff.

I tried to get the money back, crying that I was saving for new shoes for school.

Bobby had run off, taking my money and making a deal to buy what he wanted for thirty but paying double for the next hit. Then, the next morning, I'd woken up to find my shoes sliced open at the toes.

Bobby told me they'd be better now like that because I'd always have room to grow.

When my father heard about it I got duct tape for my shoes and another smack for whining. Bobby got kicked.

I'd gone to school with bruises the next day and everyone looked the other way. The family that hired me never talked to me again. It was the first time I realized just how alone I was.

There'd never been backup for me when I was a kid. Now?

Now I kept my eyes on my brother, ignoring the shadows and praying to whoever might be listening that I would survive the night.

The boat swayed gently but unevenly as we got on board. There was a slight dip as if someone had jumped onto the dark foredeck, but there was nothing to see in the darkness except the city lights and the few other boats in harbor.

"Go down," my brother ordered, pointing to the yellow light coming up from the lower deck.

Lips pressed into a thin line of resignation, I went down the steps, breathing in air fetid with the smell of unwashed brothers, cigars, and something sickly sour. I heard the sound of chewing tobacco being spat out before I turned into the cramped little galley with the tiny table and benches.

My father sat there, as big and ugly as I remembered. Broad shoulders bare under a sleeveless white shirt stained by sweat and years of greasy meals. Beau sat beside him, a few less scars, a bit more hair, same grim expression. Dawson sat at the end of the bench, leaner than Beau and less filthy than Bobby, but the look on his face was the same scowl as everyone else in the room.

"Well, well, well..." My father spit out more tobacco into a little tin can on the table. "If it ain't little miss Too Big For Her Britches. We heard you were earning a pretty penny playing mermaid for some rich boys. Did they like touching your tail?"

"I got paid to do a birthday party for a six-year-old," I said in a cold voice. "And I haven't been paid yet so I can't give it to you."

Bobby tossed the packet on the table.

My father raised his eyebrow. "This is all your brought me?"

"It's all you need. It's not like they had their bank account numbers laying around. This is there schedule for the rest of the summer. Contact information. Current projects. All of it. That's what you wanted, wasn't it? To beat them to their hauls."

"I want them dead," my father muttered, "but quiet'll work." He flipped through the paperwork, passing some of it to Dawson.

Beau and Bobby didn't have the brains for whatever was happening. That was never a good sign. Dawson was the clever one.

When he wrinkled his nose with a tiny shake of his head, I tensed.

My father clicked his tongue and pulled out a pair of reading glasses. "See, I know this one is bad. It's over in a protected area. No shipping."

"The company does charity work with the reefs. Madeleine told me about them the other day."

"Beau?"

My oldest brother stirred, glanced at the paper, and frowned. "Might be. The Amelia girl I was with said something about reef restoration."

"It's on the company website if you don't believe me," I said.

There was a low thunk from the upper deck, like something had been dropped up there by an unseen extra person.

"Dawson?" My father jutted his chin to the doorway.

With a nod, Dawson snaked past and headed to the upper deck.

"Is this what you wanted?" I asked.

"It's a start." My father handed the papers to Beau to put away. "I'll want more."

"I won't have access to more."

"You have access to Amelia," Beau said. "She's desperate for attention. Give her some validation, tell her she's important, and she'll do what you want."

I shook my head. "Won't work."

My father's scowl threatened bruises. "Why not?"

"I don't work with Amelia any more. I'm not on this cruise because I'm done working as a mermaid. The company has me doing training over in Perth next year."

Beau slammed his hand on the table. "What'd you go and do that for?" His glare would have made me shake in my thongs[33] a few years ago.

Now, I glared back. "Because I was living my own life. Making choices that benefited me. Developing my career. Being happy. You know, all those little things I should be doing with my life. Are you going to congratulate me like a real brother, or just keep sneering?"

Up on the deck there was a shout.

Bobby swore and hurried up to see what was going on with Dawson.

"We're done here," I said. "You have what you asked for."

"Where do you think you're going?" my father growled as I walked toward the stairs.

"Home," I said.

"What?" he bellowed. "You're my daughter! I own you!"

"I'm a human being!" I stepped toward the stairs. "Nobody owns me."

He gave me a look that used to make me cower.

This time, I ran. Sprinting up the stairs, I ran across the deck and the gang plank.

I was halfway down the dock when I heard laughter. The suspicious, joyful laughter of my family realizing they'd won.

Heart sinking I turned and saw what I never, ever had wanted to see in my life. My father was holding Marcus' arm.

---

[33] Thongs = flipflops in Australia.

"Come on back, Janey," my father called. "Or this little Dupre boy is going to have the worst night of his life."

"Let him go!" I shouted back.

Marcus wasn't supposed to be involved. He was going to drop me off, see which boat my family was on, and get out to call the police. Not stay. Not snoop around. Certainly not get caught.

He was a Dupre! He'd snuck on boats thousands of times. He should have vanished into the night, but he'd stayed.

Because I'd stayed. I was certain of it. Marcus had gone on board to make sure I stayed safe.

"You come here and do as your told, and I won't harm a hair on his head." My father sounded sincere, but he always did, lying or not. It already looked like Marcus had been worked over. There was blood on his mouth and his arm was hanging at an odd angle.

Bobby's laugh turned the night air sickly with the promise of violence. "Come on back, or I get to play with him. He owes me."

"Go!" Marcus shouted, sounding out of breathe. "Get out of here!"

My father punched him in the stomach and Marcus doubled over in pain.

"Call the police!" My father laughed. "Go ahead and tell them right where you at."

My brothers cackled.

"Come on home, girl," my father said. "Ain't no one else going to help you. Ain't nowhere for you to run. You come be a good girl, do as I say, and maybe you won't have two broken legs by the new year." He cuffed the back of Marcus' head. "Take him below decks."

I stood alone on the dock, watching them haul Marcus away, torn between the future I wanted and the reality I was in. If I ran, I could go on, change my name again, get another job, and keep running. Eventually, one day, maybe I'd find safety and happiness. But, even if I called the police right now, I'd lose Marcus. My father would vanish with him and Marcus would be fish food.

If I went I'd lose my future, but there was a chance—small but significant—that I could get Marcus out of this alive. He'd be able to go home to his family, live his life, do everything he wanted.

Only one of us was likely to survive.

Closing my eyes, I cursed. And then I walked back to the ship.

Marcus had people counting on him. People who cared about him. He needed to get back to them. Even if it meant giving up my future to save him.

THUNDER RUMBLED IN THE DISTANCE AS THE BOAT MADE RECORD time out of the harbor. Whatever the old tub looked like, the engine was something expensive and fast.

The air was humid, almost clingy and chill despite the heat of the summer day. In the distance, the lights of Sydney faded and an ominous silence fell around me, disrupted only by the occasional curse.

My brothers moved with more efficiency than I could have ever imagined as I sat near the diving gear. There were weight belts, dive tanks, something that looked like it might be a metal detector, and float bags.

Lots of float bags.

The kind you could fill, inflate with air from your dive tank, and that would bob to the surface with GPS tracking. I'd seen them before in safety videos about how lost passengers could be recovered, but I had a sinking feeling that whatever my family was trying to recover, it wasn't someone in distress.

But it would probably be distressing.

Cursing like a sailor under my breath, I wondered how it had all gone so wrong so fast. It had taken me years to escape my family. Plotting. Planning. Working my tail off just to save enough money to get me across the state lines and to somewhere safe. And, like a fin-flipping drug addict, all it took was one wrong step and I was right back where I began. Right here. In the middle of it. Held hostage by the fear of pain.

And because there was an actual hostage this time.

Uncurling a little, I looked over to where Marcus was laying still on the deck. He was breathing, but he wasn't moving. Or fighting.

I could remember him in fourth grade getting hit by a backpack with a rock in it, and he'd gotten up, growling and punching. Now he lay still, curling around his stomach like he was bleeding internally.

"Marcus?" I whispered, hoping my brothers were too focused on their goals to think what mine might be.

His dark eyes opened, almost glittering in the moonlight, and met mine. "You okay, cher?"

"I've had better holidays."

"Haven't we all." With a grumbling sort of sigh, he rolled into a sitting position.

I glanced up, looking for my brothers. Dawson seemed to have a grudge and I didn't want him near either of us. Giving Marcus another look, I lifted my chin as I asked, "You okay?"

He raised an eyebrow as the corner of his mouth lifted in a familiar smirk. "Cher, have I ever been knocked down by a fight?"

"You were laying pretty still."

"Your brothers aren't the pretty ones in the family. I don't want their attention."

I rolled my eyes as Marcus chuckled.

Beau thumped toward us as a plan slowly formed in my mind.

"Beau!" I shouted. "I need to use the head."

"What?" He stopped and scowled down at me.

"The head," I repeated. "The little girl's room?"

"I know what a head is."

"I need to use it. You going to throw a tantrum over that and make me pee here?"

He rolled his eyes. "Lower deck. Go down and get yerself back up here in a hurry. You get in the way, you get what's coming to ya. And you," he pointed a finger at

Marcus, "shut up." He cuffed Marcus, bouncing his head off the metal siding of the boat before stomping off.

"Oww." Marcus shook his head and looked worse for the wear.

"Stay here," I told him. "I'm going to see if I can find a phone or something."

The boat rocked beneath as I went below decks. What I wanted wasn't the bathroom, it was the engine. We had a lot of training meetings aboard the cruise ship. Things like how to tell an engine was in trouble, how to evacuate passengers, how to handle broken machines.

Training happened regularly and the people running it got bored easily, so the disasters changed every time. Meaning I'd not only learned how to efficiently load a lifeboat, I'd also learned how engines broke.

Upstairs, I heard yelling as heavy waves rocked the boat.

"Engine," I whispered to myself. "Get to the…"

There it was.

Like I'd suspected, my brothers had an older boat, but they'd taken out part of the lower deck and installed a larger engine. It meant that they could move faster than expected, but it took up a chunk of what had probably been a bunk room at some point. It also meant the engine was exposed.

More cursing from the upper deck sent dread through my spine.

"Flip this all." I snatched a work glove from the shelf, grabbed wires, and pulled.

The engine sputtered and started smoking.

Tossing the glove back where I found it, I hurried back upstairs.

Beau's glower was enough to send me running to the foredeck where I'd been.

Heavy waves rocked us to and fro. Somewhere in the distance thunder grumbled, threatening enough to send a chill down my spine.

"What did you do?" Marcus asked in a whisper as I sat back down next to the SCUBA tanks.

I shrugged. "Went below decks for a minute?"

His eyes narrowed. "Why do I smell smoke?"

Sniffing carefully, I shook my head. "I don't smell any-thing."

His dark eyes filled with worry.

"You can swim, can't you?"

"Better than you can imagine, cher." His lopsided grin was heartening. His words, not so much.

Right now I couldn't imagine anything but our impending doom.

There was a shout from the aft of the boat. A familiar, fetid fear washed over me as I heard my brothers arguing and my father's basso rumble putting them all in line again. He was angry, but they were useful, which meant he'd turn his anger elsewhere.

Heavy stomps echoed my fears, bringing back thousands of memories of nights like this back home. Nights where my father's temper turned to me as an outlet. Nights where it was my fault my father hadn't gotten what he wanted.

"It's okay," Marcus said quietly.

"It's not." I wasn't tied up, but I couldn't move. Could barely think.

My father stomped into view with Dawson and Bobby in tow as the clouds roiled behind him, cutting off the moonlight and making the night seem colder. "So. You brought me a bunch of hooey, little girl."

"I brought you what I could find." In the storage cage next to me the weight belts slid, bumping my shoulder. "What are you even looking for?"

"He knows." My father nodded to Marcus. "Don't you, Dupre? Bet you came looking for it yourself."

"Knows what?" I demanded.

Snickering, my father's smile grew. "The *Queenie* sunk not far from here, didn't she? Back in October. Big ol' ship.

I nodded slowly. "That was in the news. It was a cargo ship carrying eucalyptus wood and kangaroo pelts."

My father's disgusted look was everything I remembered it being. "Pelts?" he asked. "You think they did a search for pelts?"

"They did a search for survivors."

"They did a search for missing gems," he corrected, focus turning back to Marcus. "A museum in Thailand had a display. Jewels of the Java Sea. Crown jewels of everywhere near them."

That sounded familiar too. Amelia and I had gone to the exhibit when we'd had shore leave in September. The robbery had happened when we were sailing south near Belitung Island, headed for Jakarta.

"Someone paid for that work," my father said. "But the someone who got the jewels wasn't the someone who paid for 'em. So, *someone* ain't so happy."

Glancing at Marcus, a cold fear crept into my bones. "You think Marcus' kin knew about it?"

My father did a facial shrug, eyebrows up as his lower lip jutted out. "Makes sense, don't it? Why else would he come all the way down here when he oughta to be with family?"

Underneath us the ship rocked as the winds picked up, sending a heavy wave that broke across the deck. There was an oily, smoky smell in the wind.

The deck beneath me felt warm where my body touched it. Something down there was burning.

"Now he's here," my father said. "So, Marcus my boy, you're going to show us where your family is hunting that treasure."

Marcus laughed. "Oh, hell naw, old man." He stood up. "First, I'm here to see the kinfolk for the holidays. We're not after no treasure. Second, if there *was* treasure, there'd be no way I'm sharing with the likes of you. Yer nothing but greedy thieves."

"Name someone in your family who ain't one too!" my father demanded.

"We're good, law-abidin' folk." Marcus' accent was thick and warmed me like a good blanket. "We do salvage and rescue, and we do it well. If we were hunting that wreck—and that would be a pretty big IF—we'd be doing it because some government was paying us to. We don't play with stolen cargo or the black market. Grandmere would never let us."

The sneer on my father's face made me jump to my feet.

"Don't hurt him," I said.

My father turned to me, confusion in his eyes even as his cheeks darkened with rage. "Did I tell you to talk?"

"I'm not a pet dog," I snapped back. "I'm a human being. I get to talk when I want to. You want something obedient, get yerself a coonhound."

He blinked at me in surprise.

"Pa!" Beau shouted. "We got trouble!"

My father looked over his shoulder, obviously torn between beating me and beating my brother.

"We need to make for port before this storm coming in wrecks us," I said. We wouldn't make it that far, but closer to port I had a better chance of swimming to safety than out here, miles off shore.

"This?" My father chuckled. "This ain't nothing but a bit of wind. It'll blow over in an hour. But we're going tonight to get the goods. You can help. Or you can sit there and pout like the whiny brat you are. But, either way, he's telling us where the goods are. Once we have them, we'll be set for life. I ain't letting a dirty, backwoods Dupre steal a future from me and my boys." He nodded to my brothers. "Take him aft and get those coordinates off of him."

I wanted to scream. To fight. To do anything. But I stood there, silent and scared, the same way I always did.

Dawson stomped past me, unlocking the gear storage and grabbing a weight belt. "This'll knock sense into him."

Rain fell down in a sheer wall, drumming on the deck, killing my plans for an engine fire to save the day.

I heard shouting out of sight.

Crouching down, I ran my fingers over the cage holding the diving gear. There was a tiny personal rebreather in there under the weight belts. Grasping it deliriously I pulled it out to check the charge. Empty.

The sound of a gun cracked the night air.

For a moment the whole world fell silent. Even the rain seemed to freeze mid-drop.

There wasn't a splash, but when Dawson appeared on the edge of the pool of light, smiling, I knew Marcus was gone.

My heart sank.

The rest of my family followed Dawson as the ship rocked under the barrage of the storm.

"Get up to the helm," my father ordered. "You were around that bastard long enough. You've got to know something."

"No." I stepped toward the edge of the boat.

"You want to go with him?" My father nodded to the roiling ocean.

Behind him I saw oily flames licking a box I was almost certain had guns in it.

My father stepped forward. "Get over here! Do as you're told!"

For the first time in decades, I smiled at my family. "If my choices are to go with you or sleep with the fishes, then I'm choosing to get in bed with Davey Jones."

I threw them a rough salute that ended with one middle finger in the air, and stepped back into nothingness.

Cold water crashed around me.

Please, please let this work, I silently prayed to what-ever spark of the divine was in the frigid ocean waters. My fingers touched the three weight belts I'd hastily hidden under my shirt. Enough weight to drown me.

Violent red light flashed overhead as the fire found fuel.

A furious haze of lightning outlined the jagged edges of the boat. Debris flew, maybe my brothers trying to hit me, maybe the storm had actually done damage. It didn't matter.

I sank away from the wreckage.

Bubbles escaped as the water pressure built around my ears. My lungs started to burn. Something far too soft to be wreckage bumped my knee.

Another light flared high above as I sank.

At least I could say I went out with a bang.

Something swift moving and silky brushed past my feet.

Crocs. Sharks. Half the fish in the reef were probably circling.

My lungs burned, begging for air.

Everything was growing misty. Diluted.

I blinked, fighting for one more second of life. One more view of the world.

A shark tail was silhouetted against the distant surface lights.

Slapping a hand over my mouth and nose, I fought the urge to try to breathe. Fought against the need for air.

A white light bright as a searchlight pierced the dark-ness and I thought I saw Marcus in front of me, dark hair waving in the currents.

Strong hands caught me. I felt almost weightless, as if the belts I was wearing were cut away. Warm lips pressed against mine.

I breathed it in. This was heaven, and I knew I didn't belong.

I wasn't Little Miss Easter at the parish church. I don't think I'd even made it to a Christmas mass in my life. The best I'd ever hoped for was to wind up in a different Hell than my father. But this? This I'd fight for.

Heaven was delicious.

Marcus' tongue caressed my lips and I opened for more.

Closing my eyes, I sighed, ready to fade into this beautiful bliss of oblivion.

And then the taste of salty, mildew-seasoned rubber coated my tongue. Cold air hissed in, drying my mouth.

I'd admit to deserving a spot in Hell, but a bad regulator? That was a bridge too far.

Opening my eyes, I saw nothing but darkness.

The water was stiller, quieter. No flashes high above. No strange currents as debris fell from the wreck.

Something warm—no—*someone* warm.

A human arm was wrapping around my belly.

Squirming, I turned and saw Marcus. No mask. No regulator. No SCUBA gear at all.

Panicking, I took the regulator out of my mouth, trying to press it to his lips.

He blew a bubble that engulfed me and I swear I heard him say, "Put it back. I don't need it."

Death was officially weirder than I'd ever imagined.

LIGHTNING ARCED ACROSS THE MIDNIGHT-DARK SKY ABOVE THE crashing waves. I caught a glimpse of fish above me, and a shark tail swishing behind Marcus, but nothing seemed to be chasing us.

Closing my eyes against the sting of the saltwater, I let the current, or Marcus, or whatever was holding me here in this twilight realm between life and death, propel me forward until dry air broke across my face. Dropping the rebreather[34] and blinking, I rubbed my eyes and looked around.

We were miles from the ship, somewhere north of Sydney, with the storm visible south of us. Bright moonlight reflected off the water all around so that it seemed like there was a hazy, ethereal glow to the night.

I scrambled up a rock to safety as I tried desperately to make sense of the situation.

Marcus treaded water in front of me. Or...

Water flipped as a shark tail splashed behind him. Except, that couldn't be right, could it? If there were a shark that close to him, Marcus would have noticed.

"You're scowling, cher," Marcus said with a laughing smile.

"How..." I held out my hand toward him. "You didn't need the rebreather. You were shot, I'm pretty sure. Thrown overboard unconscious, or close to it. There's a

---

[34] Yes, we fetched it later. I wasn't polluting, I was panicking.

shark tail—looks like a black-tip—and there's no shark face. There's you."

Swimming to a nearby rock, Marcus hauled himself out of the water. Gorgeously muscled arms, lickable abs, and a tail. A mermaid tail, if the mermaid had over four feet of tail. And that was before the caudal fin.[35]

Logical explanations escaped me.

"Am I dead?" I asked.

"Cher?" Marcus laughed again as he shook his head. "No, you're alive."

"Is this a head injury of some kind? I'm unconscious? Dreaming? Hopefully going to the hospital?"

He slipped into the water and swam over. "Does this feel like a dream?" Strong fingers touched my thighs, traced over my hands, reached for me...

I leaned in, letting Marcus cradle my face so I felt the warmth of his hands. My eyes fluttered closed as I let myself soak in the peace of the moment.

"Should I kiss you?" His voice was a whisper I could barely hear over the waves around us.

Opening my eyes, I met his gaze. "Please?"

Warm lips met mine, promising everything, erasing decades of misery. Time seemed to stop. All that mattered in the moment was Marcus. His lips against mine. The taste of him when his lips parted. Strong arms wrapping around me and lifting me up.

A wave splashed my face, breaking the moment.

I pinched myself. It hurt.

Marcus frowned at me in confusion. "Something wrong, cher?"

"I'm waiting to wake up."

"You're not asleep. I can promise you dat. You're all sorts of warm and awake." And his smile said he was

---

[35] The foot part of the tail. The tail part of the tail? I don't know how to explain it without a diagram.

confident he'd helped keep me all kinds of alert.

I ran my hand down his chest and stopped where the edge of a mermaid tail would be. There was no break. No silicon. No fabric. Only human skin melting into the sandy feel of shark skin.

"There's no break," I said out loud, my hands wandering around his waist.

Marcus snorted a laugh as he dodged my touch. "That tickles!"

"You shouldn't be able to feel anything through a mermaid tail!"

"Not a plastic one," he agreed, still smiling.

"What"—I patted the tail—"is this? What is it? It looks real!"

"It is real!"

I shook my head. "It can't be!"

"Why not?"

"Because, if it's real, then you're a mermaid!"

Marcus glanced down at his tail and then looked back at me. "Yes."

"No!" Rolling my eyes in exasperation, I shook my head. "Mermaids aren't real. They're, like, flying lizards and happily ever afters. They're fairytales."

"Flying lizards are real," Marcus argued. "Agamid Lizards. You can find them all over Asia and Africa. Australia too. They have skin between their legs so they can glide."

"What?" I stared at him.

"Dragons are real!" Marcus insisted. "I did my science report on them in tenth grade!"

Giving up on a sensible argument, I splashed him with water.

Marcus laughed. "Are you mad you aren't the only mermaid in town, cher?"

"Make it make sense!"

He shrugged, and pulled me closer. "Why's your hair got red in it?"

"Genetics."

"There ya go. There's yer explanation. We was born this way. Ever since forever."

"You are telling me mermaids are real and no one noticed?" I didn't even try to keep the skepticism out of my voice.

"Lots of people noticed. There's books, movies, poems, all sorts of nonsense about merfolk."

"But no science," I argued. "Nothing in museums."

Marcus' shark tail splashed in the water. "I'm cartilaginous, suga'. There's no bones in there. Same as sharks."

"Why don't you have a mammal tail that goes up and down instead of one that goes side to side like a fish? Are you a mammal?"

He nodded. "I'm as human as you. I simply..."—he shrugged and gestured to his tail—"...have extra tanning options?"

"That's more than a tan!"

For the first time in my life I saw Marcus Dupre look hesitant. His arms slipped away, leaving me exposed to the chill of the night air. "Is this a problem, cher?"

My eyebrows went up. "Is what a problem? You having a shark tail when you swim? Yes. It makes me question my sanity and whether or not I have brain trauma. I'm terrified I'm dying right now and don't know it."

"If it's not brain trauma?"

I stared at the shark tail under me and tried to wrap my head around it. "It's still a little weird," I admitted. "But I'm not mad about it."

"Can you accept it?"

"Isn't that like asking if I'm okay with the sky being blue or the grass being green? My opinion isn't going to change your skin color any more than it's going to change who you're attracted to or—"

"I'm attracted to you," Marcus said, swimming closer. "Was that not clear?"

Waving a hand between us, I ignored the interruption. "What I was saying was... it doesn't matter. If you have extra bits and pieces, that's just how you were born, I guess." Several conflicting mythologies bounced around my stress-addled brain. "Is it? Or is this a curse or something? You said it was DNA. So I'm thinking it's how you were born."

He tilted his head. "You need sleep."

"I need... a lot of things." The reality of the situation snuck up and slammed into me.

I was sitting on a rock, in the middle of some random bay, with a mermaid—merman?—in the middle of the night. No boat. No car. No phone. No rescue in sight.

"I guess it's a good thing you aren't the kind of mermaid who lures people to their death." I sighed.

"Eh..." Marcus shrugged, his eyes sparkling with devilment.

My eyebrows went up in question.

"You're safe," he promised quickly. "Your father and brothers?" He shrugged casually. "Do you want them to be safe?"

"Not really," I admitted. "I wasn't planning to murder them, but keeping them safe isn't a requirement either. I just want them out of my life forever."

"That can be arranged."

"I also want to get back to the land. Get a shower. Sleep in a comfortable bed tonight."

"Any plans for tomorrow?" Marcus asked.

I shook my head.

"Do you think I can convince you to go on a date with me like you've promised so many times?"

The possibilities opened up in front of me like a holiday present I'd forgotten to unwrap. "I'd like that a lot," I said. "Maybe we can start with breakfast together and see where the rest of the day goes?"

BREAKFAST TURNED OUT TO BE GRUMPY DONUTS ON THE WAY home, not very auspicious. I crashed hard, then called Amelia. It was going to take some work to rebuild our friendship, but it was worth it.

So it wasn't until the following day that Marcus showed up at my apartment door before seven, bright-eyed, bushy-tailed, and grinning like the shark he was. Although the smile might have been because I was wearing an oversized t-shirt with a lemon shark on it and not much else.

"What are you doing here this early?"

"Taking you to breakfast! Come on!" He held out his hand, the blue in his dark eyes glittering like sunlight seen from the bottom of the bay.

Laughing, I pulled on a cute dress with yellow hibiscuses, ran a brush through my hair, grabbed my little lemon shark purse[36] and let Marcus kidnap me for breakfast. I spent the whole early morning drive trying to guess where we were going, but Marcus refused to give me more than smiles.[37]

We eventually pulled into a small parking lot near a port full of smaller ships. It felt uncannily familiar, but the sun was shining, the day was bright, and Marcus was with me. That last bit was the selling point.

---

[36] A yellow, lemon-shaped purse with five gills and pale eyes, not a purse shaped like an actual lemon shark, which would have been fun but much, much bigger.

[37] And a kiss at a particularly long red light.

"This way!" He led me to a set of wooden stairs on the outside of the building.

"Where are we going?"

"To have some truly amazing ricotta pancakes and a view of the harbor at dawn."

As a smiling waitress opened the door to a cozy looking cafe with a giant magnolia mural painted on the wall and the smell of fresh pancakes, I raised an eyebrow. "Sunrise was before six."

"It's close enough." Marcus put his hand on my lower back and turned to the waiter standing at the welcoming kiosk. "A seat for two with a view of the harbor, please."

The young man smiled. "Right this way."

Marcus' infectious grin spread ear to ear.

"All right," I said. "Keep your secrets."

"Not for long, cher. Not for long." Marcus held my chair for me at a glass table with a vase of yellow orchids. "Just you watch."

"Watch what?"

He nodded to the harbor then sat down across from me.

I looked out over the small boats and saw a police boat coming in. In tow behind it was a wreck of a boat that had obviously suffered fire damage. My eyes went wide.

Marcus' grin grew wider, if that were possible.

"Is that what I think it is?"

"Justice. Slow but sweet."

A blonde waitress stopped by the table, smiling sweetly and offering us fresh-squeezed orange juice.

We ordered ricotta pancakes, and Marcus got something with salmon and avocadoes.

As the waitress vanished, the police ship came into dock beneath us. There were no sirens, no fanfare, only the simple off-loading of convicts.

"They survived," I said quietly as I watched my father and brothers marched off in handcuffs.

"They did." Marcus' eyes glinted with quiet rage. "But they won't be bribing their way out of this."

I fidgeted nervously with my napkin. "What about me? They'll tell the police I helped them. I'll be carted away too."

"You?" Marcus shook his head. "Cher, last they saw of you was you jumping in the water. They bring you up, and they'll be lookin' at murder charges."

"But I'm not dead."

"No, and if anyone asks, you were with my kin here that night. The whole time." He turned his phone on, flipped through a few pages, and then handed it to me. There were pictures of us together, all dated so both times I'd run into my family I was shown being with Marcus. He leaned across the table. "Cher, you're family. You know our secrets."

I turned the phone off and slid it back to him. "How many of your family are... like you?"

"Most of them."

"Robyn?" I asked.

"Madeleine isn't. Her husband is. Robyn may be. Or she may wind up being a secret one, someone with the genes but not the looks. She heals faster when she's in the water. In time, she might find her tail. If not—" Marcus shrugged. "Kin is kin. She still belongs with us."

"But that's what she was all upset about?"

Marcus nodded. "Most little ones have their tails by now. But not all. I didn't get mine until I was nine."

The waitress appeared with a 'Complimentary Breakfast Snack' of tiny flowers made of sweet potatoes, plus a worried gaze for the police downstairs.

Looking down, I saw my father and brothers carted away. Finally answering to justice.

"It woulda been easier to let them stay lost at sea," Marcus said.

"Let the sharks have them?" I guessed.

He shrugged. "It would make life simpler."

"True, but *simple* isn't what life's about. It would have been simpler to keep my mouth shut as a kid. Or to find someone else to fight my battles. Or to run away when I saw you at Robyn's birthday party. Building my own life, finding a job I enjoyed, getting an education, choosing a life for myself..." I shook my head. "That wasn't simple. But it was the right choice."

Marcus reached across the table and took my hand. "What about loving me? Is that simple?"

"No." I shook my head as I smiled. "That's complicated too. But it's worth it. I didn't fall in love with you for simple reasons."

His eyebrows went up in surprise. "You love me?"

"I do." I nodded, my eyes tearing up a little as I realized what I was saying. "I love you for a lot of complicated reasons. Not just because you're handsome, or because you were willing to help me. But because you understand me. You love me even though you know I'm not perfect. I can see us riding out the storms of life together. I know you'll have my back when things get hard. You won't leave me."

"No, I won't." He gave my hand a squeeze then pulled away as the waitress brought our breakfast over.

Smiling, I tried the ricotta pancakes. "Delicious!"

Marcus smiled back at me.

"This is a fun first date," I said. "Breakfast and a show." I raised my glass of orange juice. "Here's to many more bright and beautiful mornings."

"And many warm nights." Marcus lifted his glass and winked at me.

Laughing, I finished breakfast as a beautiful life full of surprises stretched before me.

I finally had everything I'd always wanted. I was loved. I was protected. I was safe.

And, most importantly, I was understood by someone who knew my past and still loved me.
The future was bright indeed.

ABOUT THE AUTHOR

IF YOU ASK, LIANA BROOKS WILL TELL YOU SHE HAS A VERY ordinary life. Her daily routines include driving kids to school, cooking meals, writing books, and reading. Truly, all very ordinary things.

If you ask about the scars on her hands, Liana will happily tell you about the moray eel named Baby who bit her while she was hand feeding it for a lab experiment, or about the bite marks from a small shark while she was SCUBA diving off the coast of California, or a very vicious basketball game. Those stories are all true too.

If you ask where she lives, Liana might say Florida, Alaska, California, South Carolina, or Seoul in the Republic of Korea (South Korea, for the Americans). And she has lived in all those places.

If you ask her about her books, she'll tell you they're all wonderful. And they are! The *Fleet of Malik* books are perfect for readers who want a series of connected sci-fi romances about rebuilding after a decades-long war. If it's the enemies-to-lovers trope you're after, try the super-hero series *Heroes and Villains*. The *Time and Shadows* time-travel murder mysteries are wonderful for anyone more interested in a body count and crime than romance (though there's a bit of that as well). And the *All I Want For Christmas* series is an excellent escape into holiday romances that don't involve loving Christmases, moving to a small town, or giving up on your dreams.

You can find out more about Liana at her website, www.lianabrooks.com.

MORE BY LIANA BROOKS

Who needs kisses when you could have a werewolf?

Available from all major retailers.

ALL I WANT FOR CHRISTMAS IS A WEREWOLF

There was mistletoe over my desk. Honest to goodness mistletoe hanging over the remains of my Halloween festivities. The Great Pumpkin was now overshadowed by a hemiparasitic shrub.

When I'd left for a conference two hours ago, my desk had been a bastion against the winter holidays. A snow-free island in an otherwise elegantly decorated office suite dedicated to art.

The gallery's front foyer with the dark wood paneling and over-stuffed pine-green tub chairs was now displaying glass-and-metal snowflakes in dazzling designs.

The main negotiating room, with the long table suitable for a fleet of lawyers, had a festive Seasons Greetings banner with pine trees and bright red birds signed by various Miami athletes.

The hall had garlands, multi-colored lights, and occasionally holiday music blaring out of incautiously opened offices.

But this?

This monstrous greenery was not supposed to touch my space.

Elegant Miami's main art gallery across the MacArthur Causeway was a glittering gem of holiday art. But over here, at the offices on Miami Beach that had been selected specifically to be near my boss's favorite house, things were toned down. This was where Elegant Miami hid the nitty gritty details of business. It was the safe space for the sales people that spent all day on the phone with overseas clients; it was the home base of the style teams who went and decorated Miami palaces with carefully curated art from around the world; it was a soulless sovereignty of the contracts office where Maureen and I made sure every jot and tittle were in place.

Tittle was one of my coworker's favorite words. It means the dot over a lower case I or J, but it sounds funny. Stuck in an L-shaped, linoleum-floored concrete bunker with two high windows that looked at the neighboring building a foot away and that always smelled of nail polish and mildew, we took our fun where we could find it.

But I drew the line at plastic Naughty Santa window clings blocking the little sunlight available. Being held hostage by forced holiday cheer was not part of my paycheck.

"Happy holidays, Del!" Maureen jumped out from behind my desk wearing a bright blue sweater with silver bells, dancing elves, and snowflakes. The bell at the end of her bright pink Santa hat with pole dancing elves jingled as she stilled.

I stared, carefully counting to ten in every language I could remember, willing the other half the contracts team to vanish. It wasn't enough. Maureen and her seasonal cheer remained where they were.

"Don't you love it? I'm going to spray some fake snow too!" She pointed around at the sad, red tinsel garlands hanging off the black filing cabinets and the tiny palm tree that was sagging under a strand of rainbow lights.

"That's really not necessary," I said carefully circling around the hazardous airspace of the parasitic plant of unwanted kisses.

What was Maureen even thinking? Who on earth was I going to kiss here? It was against my personal policy to kiss clients or married people. That left Rafael Kane, office grinch, as the only possible target of unwanted contact.

Granted, he was a hot and sexy Office Grinch, but he was also the person voted most likely to ruin a party. He didn't chitchat. He didn't get distracted. He didn't waste time talking to coworkers, going to long Friday lunches, or building friendships.

Rafael Kane went to work, smiled for his clients only, and made Elegant Miami over fifteen percent of our yearly profit. We all loved him for his sales acumen and stunning good looks, but no one around here considered him a friend.

Very early on, I'd tried.

But Rafael Kane had taken one look at me, snarled like I'd stabbed his grandma, and avoided me ever since.

Which suited me just fine.

I frowned. If Maureen thought there was any chance of an office romance, my desk would look like an ad for the Great Bridal Expo. I needed tiny white seed pearls and chiffon as much as I needed mistletoe, which was about as much as a shark needed a tuba.

My idea of a good date was streaming a good murder mystery. I liked crime shows, creepy horror movies, and all things Halloween. People joked that I was a pagan, but that wasn't exactly true. I just loved the idea of magic. It made sense to me.

I should have loved the idea of Santa, except I can't remember a time I wasn't poor, and Santa doesn't visit poor kids.

December was my own personal hell. No winter solstice bonfire would ever be big enough to burn away all my anger at the forced cheer, demand for gifts, and unseasonable expectations.

I wasn't making New Year's Resolutions, I did that on my birthday in July.

I wasn't meeting anyone under the mistletoe, I wasn't that desperate.

I wasn't going to participate in the annual gift exchange, because somehow I always wound up with the bar of soap stolen from the pay-by-the-hour motel down the street.

I would be skipping the party, hitting the white sand beaches of Miami with a pink drink in hand, and spending my three days off catching up on N.W. Gehson's *Serial Killerz* series.

Maureen moved out from behind my desk and pouted. All of five-foot-nothing, she was a cute, apple-shaped woman with sunset-pink hair and perpetually purple lips from a permanent makeup choice she made thirty years ago when she was twenty-one, drunk, and planning to be an exotic dancer all her life.[1]

In the bright blue sweater, she looked like the world's glummest Sugar Plum Fairy. She was holding a shiny blue paper with the words "All I Want For The Holidays" and a blank space for a holiday wish on it.

If I ignored the paper, I might escape further holiday interrogations.

"I... I was just trying to be nice!" A huge tear shimmered in her eye.

"I know." I patted her shoulder and tried very hard not to look at the tattoo peeking above her collar that HR insisted she keep covered during work hours. "But I don't like Christmas."

"This year is going to be different!" Maureen assured, her smile turning on like a floodlight in turtle season. "I figured out why you don't like Christmas."

"Because it's a commercial farce to celebrate capitalism?"

"No, silly! Because you're single! No one's giving you the good gifts." She winked and tried to bump me with her

---

[1] She still dances under the name Cotton Candy every other Friday down at the Sugar Strip on 4th, if you're wondering.

hip, but since her head only comes up to my shoulder even in kitten heels, it didn't quite work.

I scooted around her and into my three-sided box of an office.

There were sparkly confetti snowflakes covering the nameplate that had been a gift from one of my favorite metalwork artists.

Delinna Farmer was not a name that deserved to have snow on it. Especially fake snow.

Shaking the snow off the metal cut-out of my name, I smiled up at Maureen. "Really, Maureen, I'm fine."

"You will be!" She pulled a scroll of candy pink paper out of her cleavage so it unrolled in a long, curling list. "This is Auntie Maureen's list of acceptable bachelors in the greater Miami area."

"Maureen," I said, sitting down and giving her my very best glare, "if Rafael Kane is mentioned even once on that list, I will murder you. Right here and now. There will be blood all over your dancing elf sweater. No jury will convict me."

She rolled her eyes. "Tried that. Obviously there's chemistry there, but Rafe could have chemistry with a doorknob, so it doesn't matter." She put the list of names —written in pink and purple ink—on my desk. "Names. Numbers. Histories. Sizes."

"Siz—Oh!" I covered my mouth. "Sweet mother of pearl! Maureen! This is so invasive!" I crumpled the list up and dropped it in the recycling bin.

"A girl's got to know..."

"I do not need to know anyone's sizes!" I shouted as the door to the contracts office opened and the devil himself walked in.

Rafael's brown eyes went wide, his tan face frozen in a rictus of horror.

"I'm not participating in the company Christmas party and I'm not ordering the shirts," I said loudly, willing

Maureen to play along. Rafael might be the office grinch, but nobody gossiped as much as his people in the sales department. If he even guessed at the content of Maureen's list, I'd have every art gallery employee and intern in the greater Miami area sending me extra details.

Maureen, oblivious to the threat of Dick Pic Armageddon, crossed her arms over her ample chest. "Why not? What's wrong with the holiday party?"

"Because..." I scrambled for an excuse that wouldn't insult Maureen's party planning. "...I'm seeing someone."

Rafael snorted in amusement as he shook his head and walked to our copy machine by the door. The sales department had a better one, one that could print posters and banners, but it was broken and the sales associates had been bouncing in and out of the contracts office all week. There was nothing like the holidays to convince the obscenely wealthy to drop hundreds of thousands of dollars on art.

"Oh, sweetie," Maureen said, grabbing my arm and leaning in for a sideways hug as she ignored Rafael. "You don't need to lie."

"I'm not," I lied. "I am in a relationship. And I think it's serious. We're talking about moving in together."

From the copier Rafael gave me a look of disbelief that said, *No one would ever live with you.*

Maureen patted my hand with a tiny sigh of pity. "Let me guess. His name is Nick 'The Closer' Claus and you ordered him from the toys department at Lady Things downtown? I've met him too." Her smile was wicked. "But he doesn't count as a dinner date."

Too. Much. Information.

Closing my eyes, I focused on the filing list I needed to finish today. Anything to get the image of my middle-aged co-worker gleefully bouncing through the adult toy store out of my head.

In my imagination, she wore a frilled pink skirt that barely covered her ample thighs. I shuddered.

My only option was to lie more, or to hope Rafael would step in to help me. "Maureen—"

"No!" Rafael shouted from across the room. "No more. Not until I leave. I do not need to hear this. Let me finish. Please. Five more pages!"

Just for that I wanted to play dirty, but encouraging Maureen would give me a heart attack. There was only one course of action left…

"I'm getting a dog," I said before the dick pics became porno subscriptions in my stocking. "I've been visiting the shelters and I'm planning to adopt one over the holidays."

Maureen's shoulders sagged. "Honey, that does not count."

"A dog will be more loyal than any man will!" I drew myself up, a furious dark queen with a mask of rage perfected after years of studying every campy Halloween vampire movie ever. Morticia Addams, eat your heart out. "Probably more loyal than a woman, too. It'll love me, wait for me, and cuddle with me while I watch horror movies in December. A dog won't make me watch cheesy Christmas specials. A dog will go for walks on the beach with me. A dog will be happy eating whatever I cook—"

"A dog should have a high-protein diet."

Maureen and I both turned to stare.

Had Rafael Kane actually joined a conversation that wasn't about sales? After all these years?

"Do you like dogs?" Maureen asked politely, reverting back to Sweet Office Eccentric like a chameleon. "You've never mentioned them."

Rafael stared at the wall behind the copier as he realized his mistake. His body went rigid and I swear I saw a shiver of terror shimmy through him. He knew Maureen would never let him escape now.

"My mother raised dogs when I was growing up." He finished his copy work and turned to glare at me. "I've seen the stuff you eat for lunch, Del. Do the world a favor and stick to stuffed animals and battery-operated toys. A dog deserves better." He opened his mouth as if he were going to continue, then snapped it shut and marched out, back stiff.

Maureen hummed happily. "He has such a nice tush!"

"Maureen!" I smacked her arm.

"What? I'm married, not dead. I can look."

"We're at work."

"Quitting time was eight minutes ago. I can lust after people off the clock."

"You are a dirty old woman."

"Yes I am," she said proudly.

I rolled my eyes and remembered why I'd come back in. "I need to get my water bottles. I keep forgetting them." Nine of them sat in a row by my spare shoes.

"Oh, is that what happened?" Maureen asked. "I thought you'd decided to decorate with them. Maybe make a shrine to your beloved *agua*."

"Ha ha, funny." I grabbed a big bag with the name of a local farmer's stall on it and stuffed the water bottles inside. "The winter wonderland stuff... Can you keep it off my desk?"

Maureen pouted again.

"Please? I'll bring you some of those spiced pecans you like." If the bodega had a BOGO sale going on. If it wasn't buy-one-get-one, I wasn't sharing.

Her eyes went wide with delight. "Consider it gone. I will leave your corner a natural wasteland of bones, ghouls, and whatever that thing is," she said pointing to my Zany Zombie bobblehead.

"Thank you." I packed up and went home to research animal shelters. If I was going to be forced to participate in the holidays, I deserved to have someone who was happy to see me every day.

Surely I could get a dog for Christmas. It couldn't be that hard.

Keep reading! Head to
<u>www.inkprintpress.com/lianabrooks/
christmas/werewolf/</u>
to buy your copy now!

www.ingramcontent.com/pod-product-compliance
Lightning Source LLC
Chambersburg PA
CBHW032014180726
48283CB00008B/2679